FROM ADORABLE TO YOU

Alice L Pulley

ISBN: 978-1-0683360-0-3

For Mum

My Number One Fan

ONE

Abby Richards was not a fan of unscheduled appointments. As a busy divorce solicitor, she preferred to keep a regular appointment-free zone between noon and two o'clock in order to stay on top of her workload.

Today, those hours had been set aside to prepare for a client's mediation the following morning. That was until her assistant, Emily, had crept in during an online consultation and left a note on her desk. Someone had phoned with an urgent request and managed to persuade Emily that it was important enough to warrant an exception to Abby's unwritten rule. An appointment had been made for twelve o'clock.

There was no reason to doubt Emily's judgment, but no details had been passed on to Abby other than a name: Francis Weston. A name she instantly recognised from the distant past. Perhaps someone in his family had also had an interest in Tudor history, and had named him after the ill-fated young heir to Sutton Place.

A glance at the clock told her it was not yet ten to twelve, still time for a quick read of Emily's notes to get a better understanding of what the appointment was about.

Whatever the grounds for urgency, it was unlikely to go over the standard thirty minutes. There was a good chance that Abby would be able to get her day back on track.

She buzzed through to the outer office. 'Emily, please could I have your notes for my twelve o'clock?'

'Yes, I have the information here. I'll bring it through now.'

Abby picked up the client file from an earlier appointment and was at the filing cabinet when she heard her office door opening. 'Thanks, Emily,' she said as she slotted the file into place. 'I just hope he arrives on time.'

'He's already here,' came the reply.

Her body made an involuntary jump, startled by the unexpected sound of a strong, confident male voice. A voice that was as familiar to her as her own. How was it possible? Its owner was thousands of miles away in Toronto, wasn't he? Not here, in her office.

She spun round and there he was, grinning at her with that infectious smile she adored.

'Daniel!' she cried, unable to contain the happiness that surged through her at the sight of him. To others, he was bestselling author Daniel Stratton. To Abby, he was her childhood friend. Her best friend. And the one man who remained a constant in her life.

It had been over three years since they had seen each other in person. Over three years since he had returned for her father's funeral. She had needed him desperately at that time, and he hadn't let her down.

In truth, he never had.

They kept in touch through regular video calls, and she had become used to seeing him on a screen. Now every inch of the real thing was standing only a few feet away. Just two steps, and she was in his arms for a long-awaited hug. He lifted her off her feet and twirled her round, keeping her in his arms as her feet reconnected with the floor.

'What on earth are you doing here?' she asked, unable to stop smiling. 'I thought you weren't coming until the twentieth.'

Was it just that morning when she had turned over a new month on her kitchen calendar and marked the twentieth with a big smiley face? Her plan had been to cross off the days one by one as the time of Daniel's arrival drew closer. It had never occurred to her that events were taking place at that very moment to ensure her plan would come to nothing. But she wasn't complaining.

'I decided to extend my holiday,' he told her. 'I'm afraid you'll have to put up with me for six weeks rather than three.'

'I won't mind that at all. But why didn't you say something on Sunday?'

'I thought it would be more fun doing it this way. Plus I didn't want to give you the chance to say you were too busy to see me.'

'As if I'd ever say that. I'm so happy you're here.'

She was determined to make the most of the extra time they had together. The chicken salad she'd brought from home that morning could remain uneaten in the fridge until tomorrow. Lunch out with Daniel or lunch alone at her desk? It was an easy decision. 'Do you want to go and grab a bite to eat?' she asked.

'That's exactly what I was hoping you'd say,' he said, finally releasing her from his arms.

She picked up her bag, and they walked through to where Emily was waiting anxiously. Abby gave her a smile. 'Don't worry, it's all good. It was a lovely surprise. We're off to lunch at Luca's now, but I'll be back in plenty of time for my two o'clock.'

They stepped out of the building and into the warmth of the September sunshine. Abby slipped her arm through Daniel's, effortlessly falling into step with him as they took the five-minute stroll to her favourite Italian restaurant.

'How long has Emily known you were coming?' she asked. 'She gave nothing away. I didn't suspect a thing.'

'She would have seen my email first thing on Monday. I wanted it to be a surprise, and she agreed to keep it secret for as long as she could. When I called her this morning, she told me about her last-minute plan. I thought it was brilliant. It meant you wouldn't have time to ask too many probing questions.'

He knew her so well. Ask questions was exactly what Abby would have done if she had known any earlier. 'She must have been astonished when you contacted her.'

'I think she was. But she didn't hesitate in agreeing to my idea. All she asked for was a selfie and a signed copy of *Patiently Humming*.'

Patiently Humming was Daniel's latest novel in his popular detective series. Yet another in his growing catalogue of titles that had risen swiftly to the top of the bestseller list.

'I actually gave her a signed copy of all four. It was the least I could do. Everything went so smoothly, and that was all down to Emily.' He gave a little chuckle. 'The look on your face when you turned round was priceless.'

'I was in shock! You were the last person I was expecting to walk in.'

'My clue fell flat, then? Who else would have known about your teenage obsession with Francis Weston?'

'There was no time to think. And even if I'd had more time, I would never have guessed it was you outside having a little fun with me.' She came to a stop and turned to face him. 'But you were the only one I could have wished it would be. I've missed you so much.'

'It's been too long,' he said softly.

His blue-grey eyes locked onto hers with such an intensity, for a moment she thought there was something more he was going to say. Some secret he was ready to divulge. But his face broke into his characteristic grin once again. 'I'm starving. Let's go and eat.'

And the moment had passed.

TWO

The restaurant was tucked away down a side street, two neat boxwood spheres in weathered terracotta pots guarding the entrance. 'This is it,' Abby said. 'The food is fantastic, although the lunchtime menu is rather limited. We'll have to come back one evening so you can get the full experience.'

'We can do that,' Daniel said, opening the door for her.

Abby was greeted personally by the restaurant owner. 'It's great to see you again, Abby.'

'You too, Marco. And this is my friend Daniel.'

'Welcome to Luca's, Daniel.'

'Thanks. Good to meet you.'

They were seated at a table by the window. 'I'll have whatever you're having,' Daniel said to Abby, not wanting to waste time reading through the menu.

'Okay, so that's two warm blue cheese salads and two bottles of sparkling water,' she said, handing back the menus. 'Thanks, Marco.'

As Marco took their order through to the kitchen, Abby turned her full attention back to Daniel. 'Okay, fill me in on what's been happening.'

'What do you want to know?'

'Well, to start with, why you changed your plans. Last I heard you were about to begin three weeks of uninterrupted writing.'

'I was. But it made more sense to extend my holiday and write whilst I'm here. So I booked an earlier flight; and here I am.'

'And what did Paula have to say about that?' she asked with a knowing smile. Paula was Daniel's efficient but super-strict literary agent. Abby had heard many tales of her attempts to keep him on top of his publisher's tight deadlines.

'Let's just say she wasn't in total agreement. She seemed to think I'd be partying for six weeks rather than writing, although I insisted that would not be happening.'

'So you'll be cancelling your party, then?'

'What do you think?' he laughed. 'Despite her best efforts, Paula has absolutely no control over my private life.'

Marco returned with their salads. 'Enjoy,' he said, with a smile directed at Abby.

'Thanks, Marco,' Abby said. 'I'm sure it will be delicious as always.'

When they were alone again, Daniel voiced the question that had been on his mind since they walked in. 'I assume this is the Marco you told me about?'

'Yes, that's him. We dated for a while, but that was ages ago.'

'His food is great,' Daniel said after tasting the salad.

'But I can't say the same about his judgment if he was crazy enough to let you go.'

'You know it wasn't like that. He was looking for more of a commitment than I was willing to give. It was a mutual decision to end it.'

He leant closer to her, a cheeky grin on his face. 'Even those booty calls?'

'Honestly, Daniel, you remember everything!'

'I thrive on interesting snippets of conversation.' He tapped his index finger on the side of his head. 'It's all stored in here for future reference.'

'Well, you'll have nothing new about me and Marco to file away. We're still friendly, but that's as far as it goes. Anyway, rumour has it he's now found the woman he wants to marry.'

'Good for him. And what about you?'

'Me?'

'Still adamant you won't be giving marriage a second chance?'

'Once is quite enough, thank you.'

'You do realise that thirty-five is less than two years away,' he said, his eyes twinkling at the prospect.

He was referring to the pact they had made soon after Abby had turned eight, and he'd been nearly ten. It was the summer when she had become totally absorbed in planning her own wedding after being a bridesmaid for her Aunty Holly. Much to Daniel's embarrassment, and the amusement of everyone else within earshot, Abby had declared that she had chosen Daniel to be her husband.

Her relentless persistence had finally paid off. He agreed that if she hadn't found a husband by the time she was thirty-five – the age that Holly had been at the time – he would marry her then. It was so far in the future, he'd assumed he would be safe.

'I haven't forgotten,' Abby said, smiling at the memory. 'But since I did find myself a husband, you're off the hook.'

'And you used to be so keen. What happened to that amazing little girl with her dreams of white horses, a big sparkly dress and dancing under the stars?'

'Reality,' she said emphatically, ready to move away from the subject of marriage. 'I'd rather talk about you, not my childhood fantasies. Did you arrive this morning?'

'I did. I checked in early at The Waterfront.'

'And who else knows you're back?'

'I spoke to Mum soon after I arrived. I'll be driving down there tomorrow and staying until Sunday afternoon. Then back at the hotel Sunday night.'

The waitress, Lisa, came to collect their empty plates. 'Was everything all right?' she asked.

'Delicious,' Daniel said.

'Can I get you anything else?'

'Do we have time for coffee and cake?' he asked Abby.

'We do.' She ordered two cappuccinos and two slices of lemon ricotta cake.

'There's no need to go back to the hotel,' she told him after Lisa had left. 'Come and stay with me.' It was the arrangement they had already made for the original dates of his trip. 'You don't have to wait until the twentieth. The guest room's always ready.'

'Knowing you, I imagine it would be,' he smiled. Even as a young girl she had been very neat and tidy. Everything in its place. 'It would be great to stay with you. Do you think you can take the disruption for six weeks?'

'I'm sure I can. Just try not to take over the whole apartment.'

'Show me what my parameters are, and I'll do my best. But don't let me outstay my welcome.'

'That would never happen, Daniel. I can't wait to spend more time with you. Video calls are great, but it's not the same as being together.'

'No, definitely not.'

'So when are you planning to visit Mum?' she asked. 'I'll be seeing her on Saturday. You won't be able to come with me then, obviously. Maybe next weekend?'

'I was going to phone her this afternoon to see if I could drop in before my drive down to the coast.'

'It's still the school holidays, so I can't see her saying no to that.'

'It will be great to see her again. I can go another time if she's busy, but I wanted to get the obligatory visit to my parents out of the way as soon as possible.'

Abby gave a heavy sigh. She was about to make a comment when Lisa arrived with their order.

Once they were alone again, Daniel was the first to speak. 'Go on. Say what you have to say. I know I'm in trouble.'

'I just think you're being a bit unfair. They must be

looking forward to seeing you again after all this time.'

'You would think so, although I'm not convinced. Whenever we get together the conversation comes out stilted and awkward.'

'Maybe they can sense you don't really want to be there. But you know they're very proud of you.'

'Yeah, they are now. Now that I'm successful. But they gave me zero support when I told them what I wanted to do with my life. You must remember that.'

She remembered. His parents had been appalled when they discovered his unwavering determination to become a writer. That their dream of him following their lead and becoming the next financial wizard of the family was never going to be realised.

'I know their reaction was hard on you, Daniel, but you've proved your decision was the right one. They must regret the way they behaved and the things they said back then.'

Perhaps there was some truth in what she was saying, but he still saw his journey down to the south coast as more of a duty than a fun weekend. However, there was one way to make the trip more enjoyable. It was certainly worth a try. 'Why don't you come with me? If you're there, I'll be more relaxed and on my best behaviour.'

'But I'm working tomorrow.'

'Didn't you tell me earlier you'd never be too busy to see me?' he said, making a futile attempt to hide his disappointment.

'Yes, I did. That didn't mean taking a day off with

barely any notice. Anyway, you don't need me to hold your hand.'

'Maybe I do,' he smiled. 'I love it when you hold my hand.'

But the way he had spoken about the visit to his parents had bothered her, and her face remained sombre. 'They're your parents, Daniel. You have no idea how much time you have left with them. Please don't dwell on mistakes they made in the past.'

He could see the pain in her eyes and instantly regretted how he had been so careless with his words. His mind travelled back to when he had last arrived in England, a week before Abby's father's funeral. He remembered how he had held her close as she sobbed against him for only the second time in her life.

On the day itself she had been composed and efficient, helping her distraught mother cope with the difficulty of the occasion. But he had known how devastated she had been underneath the façade.

'I'm sorry,' he said. 'Forgive me?'

'You know I can't stay mad at you. I just wish you could appreciate them a bit more.'

'I'll try.'

Abby wasn't finished. 'Have you forgotten how they stayed in Meadow Way and commuted when it would have been easier for them to live full-time in their London flat? They did that for you, Daniel. You could have ended up at boarding school.'

'You're making me feel pretty bad.'

'I don't mean to. I just want to remind you that sometimes they did get things right.'

'I'll make more of an effort with them this time, Abby.'

'Then how about making a second visit? We could go nearer your birthday.'

He grabbed hold of one of her words. 'We?'

'Of course. I've already booked time off around then, so I could come with you. And talking about your birthday, have you finally sorted out a venue for the party? It was months ago when you sent out those save-the-date emails.'

'I know. But it won't be a huge event. I was hoping we could have it at your flat.'

'Really? That's the first I've heard of it.'

'Would you mind?'

'It's not ideal. Why not have it at your parents' house?'

'Abby, come on!'

'No, don't dismiss it straightaway. The location's perfect. And there'll be so much more room than in my flat.'

'I can't see them agreeing to it.'

She gave him a sweet smile. 'But you'll ask? Please?'

'Still the same Abby,' he laughed. He had learnt very early on that it was easier to let Abby have her own way whenever possible. 'I'll see what I can do.'

'Thank you. And trust me, they *will* say yes.'

'You could be right. But whatever happens, let's spend the majority of my actual birthday together. Just the two of us.'

'Yes, I'd like that.' Then an unwelcome thought dropped into her head. 'Now that you're here for an extra three weeks, it doesn't mean you've changed your mind about me coming over in December, does it?'

Abby's office would be closed for Christmas and New Year as usual. When Daniel heard that her mother was going on a cruise over the entire holiday period, he had invited Abby to join him in Toronto.

He shook his head at her. 'Do you seriously think, after all the lockdowns and travel restrictions we've had to endure, I would turn down a chance to spend time with you?'

'Thank you. I'm so excited about spending Christmas in Canada again.'

'And visiting me, I hope?'

'Of course!'

But Daniel was having difficulty staying awake, and he tried unsuccessfully to stifle a yawn. 'Sorry.'

'No, it's okay. You need your sleep.'

'You're right, I do. Jet lag is definitely starting to take effect.'

'It's time I was heading back to the office, anyway.'

'My treat,' he said, signalling for the bill.

As they reached the main road at the end of the narrow street, Abby turned left instead of right.

'Where are you taking me now?' Daniel asked.

'If we take the scenic route, you'll be able to see my apartment.' The ten-storey building came into view round the next corner, on the other side of the river.

'And you're on the top floor?'

'Yes. Well, part of the top two floors.'

'I look forward to seeing inside.'

Abby had moved into her new flat several months after Daniel's last visit, so he had yet to see where she was living now.

'Why don't you come over this evening if you have time?' she suggested. 'But please don't set an alarm, you need your sleep. Come over if it's not too late when you wake up.'

'How late is too late?'

'Oh, I don't know. Ten-ish?'

'I'm pretty sure I won't be sleeping for that long. I'll call you.'

They came to a stop as they reached the turning that would take Abby back to her office. She didn't want to put pressure on Daniel, but after less than two hours together she knew she would find it hard to wait another three days before seeing him again. 'Will I see you later?' she asked.

'Maybe,' he said with a smile.

It was his smile that gave her the confidence to believe that she would.

THREE

Abby arrived home just before six o'clock. She slipped her shoes off her tired feet, hung her jacket in the hall cupboard, then went through to the kitchen and made herself a cup of tea.

From the moment she left the office her mind had been going over the events of the day. She still couldn't quite believe what had happened. How an ordinary day had transformed into an exceptional one without any warning at all. To be with Daniel once again had given her a warm glow inside. They had been apart for far too long.

Her invitation for the evening had been open-ended, so she had no idea if he would be coming for dinner or not. It made sense to stick with the pasta dish she had planned; there was more than enough of everything for two. Once the preparations had been done, it could be ready in less than fifteen minutes.

However, dinner would have to wait. She spent the next hour and a half refreshing her memory on the issues behind tomorrow's mediation. It was never ideal to bring work home, but she couldn't regret spending her lunchtime with Daniel. There would be precious little time to spend together over the next few days, even if he did come over tonight.

By eight o'clock she still hadn't heard from him. Her rumbling stomach was telling her it was time to eat so she made the decision not to wait. If he was able to come over later and wanted some dinner, it would be easy enough to cook a portion for him then.

By nine o'clock she had finished her meal, loaded the dishes into the dishwasher and settled down on the sofa. But she was unable to relax completely. She found herself willing the phone to ring as if she were a teenager again, anxiously waiting for her boyfriend to call.

It wasn't supposed to be like that with Daniel. They were just friends. Friends who had a meaningful and loving connection. But, nevertheless, just friends.

She picked up a book from the coffee table and soon became engrossed in that, pushing Daniel to the back of her mind. Even so, when her phone eventually rang at about quarter to ten, she couldn't answer it fast enough. 'Hey, Daniel, did you have a good sleep?'

'I did, thanks, but longer than I expected.' Ignoring Abby's advice, he had set his alarm and been awoken from a deep sleep at half past seven. After fumbling around in the dark and finally managing to put a stop to the incessant noise, he had promptly drifted off again.

On waking for the second time, he was astonished to discover that another two hours had passed. 'I can leave now,' he told her. 'It's not too late, is it?'

'Of course not.' She knew she was never going to turn

him down, however late he called. 'Have you eaten?' she asked.

'Not yet. I thought I'd pick up a pizza on my way to yours.'

'You can if you like. Or you could eat here. I've had my dinner, but I could quickly rustle some up for you.'

'That's a much better idea. I'll see you soon.'

'See you soon,' she echoed.

Daniel arrived at the front door of the building within ten minutes, and buzzed for Abby to let him in.

'Come on up,' she said, pressing the button to release the lock. When the expected knock on her door came, she was focused on stirring the contents of a saucepan on the hob and stayed where she was. 'It's open,' she called out.

'Only me,' he called back, stepping into the entrance hall with its light wooden flooring and matching furniture; the walls painted in calming shades of aqua and beige.

There were several doors leading off from the hall, but only one that was open. He made the obvious choice and found himself in an open-plan kitchen and dining area. Walking over to Abby, he planted a kiss on her cheek. 'Do you usually leave your door unlocked?'

'No, but I didn't want a lumpy sauce.'

He stood behind her, one hand resting lightly on her shoulder, the other taking a couple of cubes of ham from a bowl and popping them into his mouth.

She tipped the rest of the diced ham into the saucepan and continued stirring. 'It's my version of a quick and easy pasta dish,' she said. 'Don't be expecting authentic Italian.'

'I'm not bothered about that. It smells delicious.' He turned towards the dining room with its balcony doors showcasing the town and the bridge at night, reflections from the lights shimmering prettily over the moving water. 'What a fabulous view.'

'Isn't it? It was a huge selling point.' As she continued stirring the sauce, she moved another saucepan away from the heat with her other hand.

'Can I help?' he asked.

'Do you want to try the pasta? It should be ready by now.'

He picked up a fork and popped a piece of fusilli into his mouth. 'I'd say that's done.'

The piercing sound of the timer was impossible to ignore. 'That's the garlic bread,' she said, stirring the pasta into the sauce. She moved herself away from the cooker, leaving Daniel to deal with the hot slices of bread from the oven.

Then she added a generous sprinkling of grated English cheddar to the pasta dish as Daniel poured two glasses of red wine.

'How's that for teamwork?' he said with a smile, passing a glass to Abby.

She returned his smile and raised her glass to his. 'To the perfect team!'

FOUR

Abby sat across from Daniel at the kitchen island, drinking her wine and watching him enjoying his dinner. He had never been a fussy eater and consequently was a delight to cook for. And he was one of those people who ate what they liked and still managed to keep to their ideal weight.

'That was great,' he said, mopping up the last of the sauce with a piece of garlic bread. 'What's for pudding?'

She shook her head at him and laughed. 'You do realise my food bill will go through the roof with you here?'

'You'll let me contribute, won't you?'

'No, I won't. You're my guest. I was just making a comment, not a complaint.'

'Then I'll take you out for dinner once a week.'

'That would be lovely.' She went to look in the fridge. 'You're in luck. There's some chocolate cake left that I brought home from work yesterday. It was Helena's birthday.'

'Thank you, Helena,' he said, raising his glass once again. 'And a belated Happy Birthday for yesterday.'

As he was finishing off the remainder of the cake, Abby went into the dining area. 'I thought you could do your writing in here. We can eat our dinner at the island like tonight so you won't have to clear the table every evening. You can have this whole area to yourself. Would that be okay?'

'It's more than okay. It's just what I need.' He came to join her, then walked over to the glass doors. 'I'm sure I'll spend some time out there, too.'

'It takes on a whole new look in the daytime. I have breakfast there if the weather's nice.'

'And I'll join you for breakfast, whatever the weather.'

'I'd like that.'

He put his arm casually across her shoulders. 'I really appreciate everything you're doing for me, Abby. It's so much better than being stuck in a hotel room for weeks.'

'It'll be great having you here. When did we last spend this amount of time together?'

There was certainly going to be a change in her routine with him staying, but she wouldn't have it any other way. The thought of him hiding away in a hotel for three weeks was not a happy one.

'As long as you're aware how moody and disruptive I can be when I'm writing.'

She smiled up at him. 'I'll cope. And just ask if there's anything else you need. I want you to feel completely at home here.'

She opened a connecting door through to the lounge, where the wooden flooring was replaced by a plush carpet. It was a cosy and comfortable room, but also elegant and stylish. A lot of thought had gone into each piece of furniture, each accessory, each picture on the wall.

'This is so you,' he said. 'It all fits together perfectly. I don't know how you do it.'

'For the first time I had a completely blank canvas so I wanted to make the flat truly mine. It took months, but I think it was worth the effort.'

'Absolutely. And more of that fantastic view.'

'Yes. I never tire of it.'

They spread themselves out on the sofa: Daniel with his shoeless feet up on the chaise longue; Abby with her legs stretched out across his lap.

'So did you speak to Mum?' she asked.

'I did. She said she would love to see me tomorrow.'

'That's great. And when will you be starting your writing?'

'Monday. I already have the outline and pages of scribbled notes, but I'll start the serious stuff then.'

'Does it have a title yet?'

He had been wondering when she would ask that particular question. '*Chaotic Contradictions*,' he said with a smile, watching her face closely, waiting for her reaction. He wasn't disappointed.

She stared at him, her face a mixture of astonishment and joy. 'That's from my poem!' The poem she had written for him in the days before he left for university. A time when he had been ready to take his first step towards becoming a published author, but she had yet to decide the path she would be taking.

She quoted the relevant line, still as fresh in her memory

as if it had been written yesterday. '"*Seeking solace from the confused chaotic contradictions of the present*". I was so proud of that poem back then.'

'You had every right to be proud. I thought it was brilliant.'

'You were a brilliant inspiration. And obviously I was heavily influenced by the game we used to play. Do you remember that?'

'How could I not?' he laughed. 'Adorable Abby.'

She thought for a moment, then said, 'Baffling Books.'

He raised his eyebrows. 'Are you referring to mine?'

'It's a compliment. If the reader knows what's going on, it rather defeats the point of a detective novel, don't you think?'

'Fair enough.' He quickly came up with a suggestion for the next letter: 'Chaotic Contradictions?'

It was no surprise when Abby objected. 'That's not allowed!'

There was a short pause before he came up with a legitimate replacement. 'Critical Catastrophes.'

'Let's hope there's not going to be one of those while you're here,' she said.

'There could be if you distract me too much.'

'Why would you say that?'

'Because *you*,' he said, tapping her once on the nose with his finger, 'can be a huge distraction.'

'No way! I'm not taking the blame for you not getting your writing done. I'll be upstairs or in here. Quiet as a mouse.'

'You'll have to let me know when you come home. I may need a reminder to stop and eat.'

'As long as you're sure.'

'I'm sure. And you're happy for me to use chaotic contradictions?'

'Yes, you must. Don't you dare change your mind!'

'I'm not brave enough to do that,' he laughed.

She removed her legs from his lap and snuggled up against him. 'Thank you, Daniel Delicious,' she said, reverting back to their game. It was no trouble at all coming up with words for that letter. When they had played the game years before, the A's and the D's had always remained the same.

'And on that note, I think it's time I left. I need to get some sleep before my drive tomorrow.'

However, she had an alternative suggestion to put to him. 'Why don't you stay here tonight?'

'It does sound tempting. But I didn't bring anything with me.'

'I have toiletries and towels you can use. Then you can go back to the hotel in the morning to change and pick up your things.'

He took only a moment to decide. 'Sounds good. Thanks, Abby.'

'Let me show you your room.'

They went through another door which led back into the hall. She opened the door on the right, revealing a fully-furnished double bedroom decorated in the same shades of aqua and beige that he had seen in the other rooms. 'What do you think?' she asked as he stepped inside.

'I think it's perfect.' He opened the door to the en suite shower room. 'Abby, this is spotless. Are you expecting me to keep it like this?'

'I'm not going to interfere at all. This will be your own private space.'

He smiled at her. 'And then you'll get it deep cleaned after I've left?'

'Probably!'

Their smiles turned into laughter, then he lifted her up and twirled her round for the second time that day. He set her back on her feet before taking hold of her hands, unwittingly sending a spark of electricity through them both. She snatched her hands back and turned away from him, feeling the colour creeping onto her face.

Her reaction hadn't gone unnoticed, but he wouldn't embarrass her further by mentioning it. 'Shall we finish off the wine?' he asked, keeping his voice light.

'Just give me a moment.' She disappeared into the cloakroom and splashed cold water onto her pink cheeks. What was happening to her? It was only Daniel. She should not be reacting like this in front of Daniel.

When she had composed herself, she found him sitting at the kitchen island, his eyes distant, his face thoughtful. As she walked over to him, his expression changed to a teasing smile. 'I was looking at your calendar. Very old school.'

'Maybe. But I find it useful.'

'Looks like something fun's happening on the twentieth.'

'That's what I thought. Until someone decided to do something impulsive and messed up my plans. Typical!'

His arm curled around her waist, drawing her closer to him. 'That's my new role in life. To bring chaos to your ordered world.'

'You think I need dragging out of my comfort zone, do you?' she asked, picking up her wine glass.

'I think it's important for us all to challenge ourselves. Who knows where we might end up?' He paused, then added quietly, 'It could be somewhere amazing.'

Once again she could sense the unspoken words hanging between them. His face was just inches away. She had a sudden urge to move forward and press her lips onto his. What was she thinking?

She took a step back, desperate to maintain her control, and brought the glass to her lips instead.

'Are you okay?' he asked.

But his voice was soft and tender when she needed it to be playful. She was unable to meet his eyes. 'I'm feeling a bit tired, that's all.'

'Then we'd better get you to bed,' he said, before emptying his own glass.

She knew he was just looking out for her. But as soon as she heard those words, she wanted nothing more than to fall asleep in his arms. Why was his presence having such an effect on her? It could only be because it had been so long since she had last seen him. Surely nothing more than that?

They walked through to the hall and stood outside Daniel's bedroom door to say goodnight. 'Can you make sure I'm awake before you leave?' he asked. 'I don't want to be too late getting up.'

'Yes, of course. I'll want to come and say goodbye.'

'Thanks, Abby. For everything. Sleep well.'

'You too.'

They had one last hug before she made her way upstairs to her own room.

It was almost one o'clock. But despite the late hour, Abby's mind was restless and she couldn't settle. She hadn't been prepared for Daniel's sudden appearance at the office. Hadn't expected such an alarming rush of emotions.

Perhaps it was just as well he was going away for the weekend. It would give her time to adjust to him being here. When he returned, they would find themselves comfortably back in the friend zone. It had to be that way. Anything else was simply out of the question.

FIVE

The six o'clock alarm unceremoniously signalled the start of a new day for Abby after only a few hours' sleep, but staying in bed was not an option for her. She always gave herself plenty of time to ease gently into the day before leaving for work. Being in a last-minute rush every morning was not what she needed.

But she was not expecting Daniel to be up at this time. She made her way downstairs in her dressing gown, her slippered feet making no noise as she crossed the hall.

Sitting on the balcony with her coffee, it felt strange that Daniel was so close and yet still out of reach. They could have enjoyed coffee and a chat, then had breakfast together. But that would have to wait until another day.

It didn't seem fair to wake him this early. If he hadn't surfaced by the time she was dressed and ready to leave, she would take him a coffee and wake him then. They could have a few minutes together before she left for the office.

By eight o'clock there was still no sign of him. Abby knocked on his bedroom door. No answer. She opened the door a little and called out his name. Still no answer.

She went in and sat on the edge of the bed, setting his coffee down on the bedside table. Then she ran her fingers through his floppy fringe, pushing it away from his eyes. 'I'm going to work soon Daniel,' she said, keeping her voice soft. 'It's time to wake up.'

'Mmm,' he murmured contentedly, his lips shaping into a lazy smile. 'Can you wake me like this every morning? Your touch is beautiful.'

'It's gone eight o'clock. I just came to say goodbye.'

He finally opened his eyes. The first thing he noticed was that she was dressed for work. 'It's that time already?' he said, propping himself up on his elbows. 'Weren't we supposed to be having breakfast together?'

'Not today. I thought I should let you sleep for as long as possible. I've brought you a coffee.'

He rested a pillow against the headboard and sat up. 'Thanks. But no time for a chat?'

'No, I'm sorry. I can't stay. I don't want to be late in.'

He put down his coffee and opened his arms. 'Not even time for a hug?'

She gave him a smile. 'Go on then. A very quick one.'

He held her in his arms for a few enjoyable seconds before she pulled away.

'Now I really do have to go,' she said, kissing him on the cheek before getting back on her feet. 'Have a good journey, and I'll see you Sunday.'

'Let me walk you to work,' he said on a sudden impulse.

'Daniel, I have to leave.'

'Give me five minutes.'

'Five minutes,' she said, swiftly exiting the room before he threw off the duvet.

He was ready in three. A quick trip to the bathroom, then he pulled on his clothes from the night before.

Abby was waiting for him by the front door.

'Will I do?' he asked.

'You'll do fine,' she said, ignoring the fact that his clothes were slightly crumpled. 'But you would have had time to run a comb through your hair.'

'Why don't you do it for me?'

She couldn't resist the invitation to run her fingers through his hair once again, this time giving it more definition.

'Do I look good enough for you now?' he grinned.

'Stop fishing for compliments,' she said, trying, but failing, to keep her voice stern. 'We have to go.'

They made their way across the bridge and into town, a walk Abby had done hundreds of times before. 'It's nice to have some company,' she said, slipping her arm through Daniel's. 'I could get used to this.'

'It's my pleasure. Does everyone arrive early like you?'

'No. Most arrive somewhere between nine and half past. I like to get there first and run through my agenda for the day while it's quiet.'

'You'd better watch out for those unscheduled appointments.'

'Please, no more of those. I couldn't cope!'

'Do you have a busy day planned?'

'I do. I have a mediation this morning with a client, her estranged spouse and his solicitor. They won't agree on anything except their refusal to be in the same room as each other. We've called in an assessor to help sort it out.'

'Then it would be pointless to try and persuade you to phone in sick?'

'Daniel, you can't ask me to do that. I won't be taking any time off until the twentieth.'

He gave a sigh. 'It was just a thought.'

'What time did you say you'd be at Mum's?' she asked.

'Half ten. I'll have time for a quick shower, grab some breakfast, then be good to go.'

'As long as you've had enough sleep.'

'Yeah, I'm wide awake now.'

They turned into a street of large Victorian houses that had been converted into offices, and stopped a few feet away from the entrance to Abby's building.

'There's just one more thing before you go,' Daniel said, pausing for effect before his next two words. He leant closer to her and whispered softly in her ear. 'Erotic Emotions.'

'Daniel!' she cried in mock horror.

'What did I do?' he said, feigning innocence. 'It's just the next letter in our game.'

'If those are the sort of words you're choosing, I might not want to play anymore.'

'You know you don't mean that,' he laughed.

'Well, I'm definitely putting you on notice,' she said,

relenting with a smile.

'So what super-appropriate words do you have for me?'

'Right now, absolutely nothing. I need to start work, and you need to get back to the hotel. You don't want to be late for Mum.'

'That is entirely under your control,' he said, wrapping his arms around her. 'Because I'm not going anywhere until you come up with your two words.'

'I'm afraid you'll have to wait until Sunday. I don't have two words ready.'

'No, that's not good enough. I'm not letting you go until you think of something.'

She thought of one word immediately. It described the state of her brain at that precise moment. As she searched her mind for the second word, an obvious one suddenly arrived. 'Frantic Flirting,' she said, relieved that it hadn't taken her too long after all.

'Not bad,' he said, keeping to his promise and releasing her. 'I'll see you Sunday. Can I call you tonight?'

'Yes, I'll be home.' She gave him another quick kiss on the cheek. 'Drive safely. And try to relax and enjoy the visit.'

'I'll do my best,' he said, giving her one last smile before she disappeared into the building.

SIX

It was a fifteen-mile drive to the village where Daniel and Abby had lived as children and where Abby's mother, Beth, still lived. Beth had worked as a teacher at the village school when they had been pupils there, but for the past fifteen years had been teaching at a bigger primary school in the adjoining town.

Less than a quarter of a mile past his old school, Daniel turned into Meadow Way. So many of his early memories were attached to this tiny part of the world. This was the street where he had spent his formative years. Where, at the end of every school day, he would race down the street with Abby to her house. And her house was where he would stay until one or other of his parents would come and collect him.

At first he had been embarrassed at being babysat when he was almost eight years old. But there had been a few get-togethers in the preceding summer holidays, and it soon became clear that it would not be so bad after all. Abby's parents had welcomed him with open arms and were always interested in what he had to say. Abby herself had been delighted at the prospect of him joining her family. She had accepted him from the start.

He had been a year above her at school, although he was almost two years older as his birthday was late September and hers was in the summer. They had stuck with their peer groups at school, but out of school they soon became firm friends.

Even after he moved to the independent boys' school in town, they had remained close. And when his parents had agreed he was old enough and mature enough to no longer need constant supervision, he still spent a lot of his time with Abby.

Just before a bend in the road, Daniel pulled up outside a four-bedroomed detached house that was very familiar to him. This was the house where he had lived until leaving for university, a few days after his nineteenth birthday. He would soon be turning thirty-five, but that time was still firmly imprinted in his memory.

Looking up at what was once his bedroom window, his mind recalled how he and Abby had sat on his bed the evening before he left, saying goodbye. That was when she had surprised him with the poem. Over time the paper had become worn through at the folds, but he still carried the poem in his wallet to this day.

It had always been his dream to become a writer, and she had been so worried that she didn't have a plan for her own future. 'What on earth am I going to do with my life?' he remembered her saying. He had seen a sadness in her eyes as she waited for him to tell her everything would be okay.

'You don't have to decide now,' he had told her. 'There's plenty of time for that. But whatever you choose to do, I know you'll make a success of it. You're amazing. You can do anything you put your mind to.' He hadn't been expecting the question, and thought he should have done better. But Abby had been happy with his answer.

The next morning his father's car had been packed to capacity – and they were ready to leave – when suddenly he heard her calling his name. She was running down the street towards him, and he had caught her in his arms, ignoring his father's unhelpful comment about the time.

'How will I ever cope without you?' she had asked, her beautiful eyes brimming with tears.

He had held her close, the sound of her sobbing tearing at his heart, and made her a promise. 'You'll never be without me.'

And it was a promise he had kept. As their lives expanded and taken different paths, gradually the weeks apart turned into months and eventually into years. But throughout those years the bond between them had remained strong. And when they did find themselves together once again, it was as if they had never been apart.

Abby had been the first person he had told when a publisher became interested in his work. The first person he turned to when he needed a sympathetic ear or when he just needed to talk. And she was always the first person he wanted to see when he came home. He could not imagine his life without her.

A twitching curtain in the bedroom window caught his

attention, bringing his reminiscing to an abrupt end. He realised he had been sitting outside his former home, lost in his thoughts, for almost fifteen minutes. Probably looking very suspicious to the current owners of the house, who would have no idea who he was. It was time to leave.

Round the corner, and a little further down, he turned into the driveway of a three-bedroomed semi-detached house that was also very familiar. A house where he was always assured of a warm welcome.

Beth was delighted to see him and hugged him tightly. They sat in the south-facing conservatory, drinking tea and eating homemade pineapple cake. 'I made it yesterday as soon as I knew you were coming,' she said. 'It was a lovely surprise to hear you'd come back earlier than planned. I'm sure your parents are looking forward to seeing you, too.'

'Mum did seem pleased to hear from me when I spoke to her yesterday,' Daniel said. 'I'll be staying there a couple of nights, then when I get back I'll be staying with Abby. I was there last night. Her flat is very impressive.'

'Yes, it's lovely. She worked hard at turning her ideas into reality. The colours and uncluttered spaces make it so tranquil and calming. Will you be writing whilst you're there?'

'Abby has been very generous and given me the dining room. I'll be starting my next novel on Monday: *Chaotic Contradictions*. The title came from one of her poems.'

'I bet she was thrilled with that,' Beth smiled. Then she reached out and took hold of Daniel's hand. 'I want to thank you again for what you did for Adam. It was very moving to see the dedication to him in *Patiently Humming*.'

He gave her hand a squeeze. 'I was proud to do it. He was an integral part of my life, and I wanted to acknowledge that.'

The conversation flowed smoothly between them for the remainder of Daniel's visit. There were no awkward silences. No hoops to jump through. He could just be himself. It was a world away from the type of conversations he had with his own parents.

'I shall be seeing Abby tomorrow,' Beth said as she walked him to the front door. 'I expect you'll be our favourite topic of conversation.'

'Oh no,' he laughed. 'Do I need to worry?'

'You do if I hear you've left a trail of broken hearts behind in Canada.' She knew from Abby that he dated fairly regularly, but there was no-one significant in his life at the moment. 'When do you think you'll be ready to settle down?' she asked.

'When the right woman agrees to have me,' he said with a smile, not annoyed by the question as he would have been had it come from his own mother.

Daniel's relationship with his parents had always been rather strained. When he was younger, he had found it hard to live up to their high expectations. They had rarely listened to his opinion, quickly dismissing his dreams as foolish nonsense. Their obvious displeasure in his career choice still rankled. His father's words had been particularly unpleasant.

But on the drive down to the coast, he remembered Abby's reaction to the way he had spoken about his visit and resolved to make more of an effort. If he changed his defensive attitude, it could be that his parents would become more relaxed, too.

And he should never forget that it was through one of their decisions that he had first met Abby. Although they could never have known how much of an impact that decision would have on his life, how could he not be grateful to them for making it?

After nearly three hours of driving, Daniel found himself outside the gates of his parents' home. The well-established trees and shrubs shielded the view of the house from the road. This was the house they had bought for their retirement, vastly different from the one they had lived in at Meadow Way. An exclusive 1930s seafront property set in formal gardens, with private access down to a small beach.

His mother kept a room for him to use on the rare occasions he stayed over, although he had never really thought of the house as home. But he could appreciate the intrinsic beauty of the location and understood why they had chosen to retire there.

He drove slowly down the driveway to the sound of gravel crunching under the tyres, and parked a short distance from the front door.

His parents, Greg and Olivia, came out to greet him as he was retrieving his bag from the boot of the car. He shook his father's hand and kissed his mother on the cheek. She gave him a hug, telling him how happy she was to see him. He had no reason to doubt her sincerity. It made him more determined to make an effort.

He wasn't expecting miracles, even if they did agree to the party. There would be no open declarations of love. No false promises of more regular contact. But it would be the first step towards building a better relationship with them. Unhappy memories of their shared past were no longer relevant. He was ready to move on.

SEVEN

'I can't believe we're back doing this again,' Daniel said as he connected with Abby for their video call on Friday night.

'I know,' Abby said with some sympathy. 'But it was a good idea to go and see your parents. I bet they were pleased to see you, weren't they?'

'Actually, they were. Particularly Mum. It's going better than I expected.'

'So you're behaving yourself?'

'You should be proud of me. I was doing some serious thinking on the drive down about what you said, and I'm losing the attitude.'

'I'm glad to hear it.'

'Although I still say it would be better if you were here with me,' he added.

'See what happens when you insist on acting impulsively? But I'll be with you next time.'

'You certainly will,' he grinned. 'Because we're having the party down here.'

Abby sat up straight when she heard this news. 'Daniel, that's fantastic. Did they take a lot of persuading?'

'Not at all. In fact, Mum was very enthusiastic about it.'

'Didn't I tell you it would be okay?'

'You did. But I hope you weren't expecting to have any input in the planning. Mum's relishing the challenge of organising everything. I've given her a list of who's coming, but she says that's as much help as she wants from me. She's downstairs right now checking out caterers and hotel rooms.'

'I'm happy for her to take charge,' Abby said. 'But tell her to let me know if she needs help with anything.'

'Thanks. I'll pass that on. She's also arranging transport to and from the hotel for those who won't want to drive. Dad would only agree to the party on the proviso that people wouldn't be sleeping over.'

'Yes, I can understand that.'

'But we can stay, obviously. And Lucy and Angus.'

Abby had met Daniel's cousin Lucy a few times when they were younger, and had been Daniel's plus one at Lucy's wedding to Angus. She hadn't seen them since, but Daniel had told her there were now two additions to the family. 'Will they be bringing the children?' she asked.

'Mum's insisting on it. I've been assured it won't be an issue. I get the impression she's taken on a grandmotherly role now that Lucy's parents have retired to Spain. She's convinced she'll never be a grandmother in her own right.'

Daniel's thoughts on having children of his own were no secret to Abby. He was adamant he would never be a part-time dad who floated in and out of his children's lives. And since he had never shown any desire to settle down, it seemed unlikely that fatherhood was in his plans for the near future.

'It'll be nice to catch up with Lucy,' Abby said. 'It's been a while. How is she?'

'Still happily married to Angus. They're not part of your doom and gloom divorce statistics just yet.'

'I'm glad to hear it. They're a lovely couple.'

'You're right, they are. They'll be coming down on the Friday and staying until Sunday, the same as us. So we'll see quite a lot of them. And on Saturday afternoon we're having a barbecue with a few close friends, most of whom you know.'

'It all sounds great. And what about your birthday?'

'I thought we could leave late morning, then spend the rest of the day together.'

'It's your day, Daniel. I'm happy to go along with whatever you want.'

He smiled at her, a mischievous glint in his eyes. 'You could well regret saying that.'

'That sounds ominous. What have you been plotting?'

'Nothing sinister. But I do have a few ideas. Maybe a long walk on the beach, take a picnic, see where we end up.'

'I like the sound of that.'

'Or book a table at a cliff top restaurant.'

'That sounds good, too.

'If the weather's miserable, we could drive straight back to your flat. Then go out and celebrate in the evening.'

'Yes, I'd be happy to do that.'

'Or we could go and get married.'

This last suggestion was spoken as nonchalantly as the rest, and Abby almost found herself agreeing to that as well. She managed to pull herself together in time. 'No way! It's you that's turning thirty-five, not me.'

'Don't remind me.'

But the constant reference to their marriage pact was becoming difficult for Abby. They hadn't spoken about it for so long, even before her marriage to Gavin, and yet since Daniel's arrival it was starting to become part of every conversation they had.

She thought she had put it behind her with all her other childhood dreams. So why did her heart flutter every time he brought it up?

'What will you be doing tomorrow?' she asked, hastily changing direction.

'I'll be letting everyone know the location and hotel details.' He paused, his mood turning more sombre. 'Then I've agreed to play golf with Dad. Should be interesting. We've not done that for years.'

'It's good you're making the effort, Daniel. You never know, you might even enjoy it.'

'Maybe. If not, it could turn very awkward, very quickly. I'll let you know tomorrow how it goes.'

But tomorrow was the first Saturday of the month. Girls' night. 'I'll be meeting up with the girls,' Abby said. 'So I'm afraid I won't be free for a chat.'

'Then we'll catch up on Sunday when I get back.' He was disappointed that she wouldn't be free. After what could be a stressful round of golf with his father, then a rehash of his performance over a drink in the bar, Daniel would have welcomed a more relaxing chat with Abby in the evening. But he could hardly expect her to put her life on hold.

It was his turn to change the subject. 'How was work?' he asked. 'Did you get your warring couple on speaking terms?'

'Not exactly, although they did eventually reach an agreement. But you were the main attraction in the office today. Emily posted her selfie with you, and we were bombarded with questions from everyone. Helena was annoyed with me because I didn't take a picture of you eating her birthday cake.'

She could see Daniel laughing. 'I thought you'd like that,' she said, giving him a smile. 'But I found it really strange to hear the way they were talking about you. I don't think of you as a celebrity. To me you're just Daniel.'

'Just Daniel? Thanks a lot!'

'I don't mean it in a bad way. You know how proud I am of you. But I see you first as my best friend, then as someone who happens to be an incredible writer. Not the other way round. Does that make sense?'

'It makes perfect sense. You're forgiven.'

The conversation continued between them for another hour, until Abby was forced to admit that she needed her sleep; it was time to bring their call to an end. But it was another forty minutes before they finally managed to say goodnight.

Daniel was still occupying Abby's thoughts the following morning. All those confused, chaotic contradictions she had written about as a teenager were with her once again, except this time they were all focused on Daniel. Her emotions were threatening to derail her. What she needed was to talk things through with someone before Daniel returned from his family visit.

Of course, she would be seeing her mother later that day. But because of Beth's close relationship with Daniel, Abby was reluctant to talk to her about the feelings that had overwhelmed her since his arrival.

She decided to message her friend Asha to ask if they could meet up an hour early. Abby and Asha had been friends since university. In fact, it was through Abby that Asha had met her husband. Rakesh had grown up only a few miles from Abby's childhood home and been a school friend of Daniel's.

Asha was the only one of their girlfriend group who had met Daniel. The only one who Abby felt she could talk to freely about their relationship.

Asha was the perfect choice.

EIGHT

By seven o'clock that evening, Abby and Asha were sitting together at a quiet table in the corner of their favourite local bar. The only thing Abby had told Asha in her message was that she wanted to talk about Daniel before Ellie and Georgia arrived.

'Is it about the party?' was Asha's first question. 'We had an email from Daniel this morning giving us the location.'

'Yes, he finally got it sorted,' Abby said.

'I googled the address, and the house looks amazing. Have you been there?'

'No, but I'm really looking forward to it. It certainly sounds a much better venue than my flat, which was his first suggestion.'

'Your flat is lovely,' Asha said loyally. 'Although, I must admit, a weekend by the sea sounds wonderful. We've also been invited to a barbecue on Saturday afternoon, so we've decided to drive down after work on Friday.'

'It'll be great to have you both there,' Abby said. 'But the party isn't the reason I asked to see you.' She was aware they had limited time, and she needed to get to the point. 'It's about Daniel arriving three weeks early. He turned up at the office on Thursday out of the blue.'

'I had no idea he was here already. But then we all know Daniel likes the element of surprise. How did you cope?'

'I was in shock. I let him sweep me off my feet. Literally.'

'And is he staying with you?'

Abby quickly filled Asha in on the accommodation arrangements. Then she hesitated. There was so much more she wanted to say. But now the moment had arrived, she found it wasn't as easy as she'd hoped it would be.

Asha wasn't fooled. Abby had told her nothing that couldn't have been said in front of the others. 'What's happened?' she asked. 'Are you okay?'

Abby took a sip of her drink, giving herself time to search for the right words to explain the situation she found herself in.

'My emotions have been all over the place since he arrived,' she said. 'I'm starting to question everything about our relationship.'

'And how is he with you?'

'Very flirty and fun, like he's always been. I would never want that to change. It's just that I'm finding it so much harder to handle than before. Then there's the physical closeness, which has been challenging to say the least. I had to fight the urge to kiss him on Thursday night. And I'm not talking about a peck on the cheek.'

'I think you've always been a little bit in love with him,

haven't you?' Asha said softly.

Abby couldn't deny it. 'I suppose I have. But as a good friend. Not in the way I loved Gavin.'

Why did she still feel the need to validate her short-lived marriage? She had met Gavin during her second year at university and married him on a trip to Las Vegas after graduation. The first and last time she had acted purely on impulse. But she would never believe they hadn't been in love.

'Oh yes, Gavin,' Asha said with a smile. 'Another guy who sent your emotions into turmoil. Honestly, Abby, you're the most level-headed person I know. But when it comes to love you're a jumbled mess.'

Abby was astonished that Asha seemed to be linking her feelings for Daniel with those she had once felt for her ex-husband. 'I can't be in love with Daniel like that,' she said. 'It would ruin everything.'

Asha thought it best not to disagree. 'Then just enjoy the time you have together while he's here and try to keep those emotions in check.'

'I wish it were that simple.' Abby went on to tell Asha about all the talk of marriage there had been between herself and Daniel. Starting on the day of his arrival when they were having lunch together, and ending with their video call the night before when he had suggested they get married on his birthday. 'He can't possibly have been serious. But it's making my head spin.'

'Imagine for a moment that he *had* been serious,' Asha said. 'What would your answer have been?'

'You know my thoughts on marriage. I've got no intention of putting myself through that again.'

'You are allowed to change your mind.'

Abby briefly closed her eyes, sighing deeply before replying. 'However tempting it would be, I could never say yes. If we tried and failed, I'd end up losing my best friend. I can't take that risk.' She paused before adding quietly, 'And yet I woke up this morning wishing he were there beside me.'

'Oh Abby. You've really got it bad, haven't you?'

'I can't be in love,' she said again. 'I don't know what's happening to me. It makes no sense!'

'Who we fall in love with doesn't always have to make sense.'

But Abby refused to accept she was falling in love with her best friend. 'No, it's not like that. It's because I haven't seen him for so long, that's all it is.'

'Why don't you tell him all the talk of marriage is making you feel uncomfortable?' Asha suggested. 'This is Daniel we're talking about. He would never want to hurt you, would he?'

'No. Never. But I'm hoping once he starts his writing on Monday, his focus will be on that. Then we'll fall back into the friend zone and settle naturally into a comfortable routine.'

'Perhaps,' Asha said doubtfully. 'Although it could be difficult having him sleeping under the same roof. Wouldn't you rather he stayed in a hotel?'

'Absolutely not!' Abby insisted, and they couldn't help

but laugh at her reaction and the dilemma she found herself in.

'I think you need to be clear in your mind exactly what it is you want from the relationship, Abby.'

'I want us to stay friends. It's the only relationship that will work.' She was not prepared to go down any other route with Daniel. To lose the close bond they had built up over decades of friendship would be unbearable.

'Then I hope it works out for you,' Asha said. 'I'm sorry I couldn't be more helpful.'

'No, you've been great. To be able to talk it through with someone was just what I needed.'

They both looked up as the sound of distinctive laughter reached them from the bar, instantly recognisable as belonging to their friend Georgia. 'How much are we telling the others?' Asha whispered.

'I don't mind them knowing that Daniel's here, but let's not elaborate on that.'

'Okay. And call me anytime if you want to talk again.'

'Thanks, Asha.'

Georgia and Ellie made their way over to the table. 'You two are looking very cosy,' Georgia said as she sat down next to Abby.

'We were just talking about Daniel's surprise arrival a couple of days ago,' Abby said.

'Your fabulous writer friend is here? Why on earth didn't you bring him with you?'

'He's visiting his parents this weekend.'

'Wasn't he supposed to be coming at the end of the

month?' Ellie asked.

'Yes, he was. But he surprised me at the office on Thursday.'

'Oh my goodness! What did you do?'

'I took him to Luca's for lunch.'

'You took him to Luca's?' Ellie laughed. 'What were you trying to do, make him jealous?'

'Of course not. Daniel's not bothered about things like that. We've always talked to each other about who we're dating.'

'Abby, you are so blasé about relationships. Are you still refusing to show any romantic interest in Daniel?'

'He's my best friend,' Abby said, wondering how it had come to this so quickly. 'There's never going to be anything more between us.'

'If you need him taking off your hands, then send him my way,' Georgia said. 'I'll show him how to have fun while he's here.'

Abby was horrified at the thought. 'I'd rather you didn't,' she blurted out before giving herself time to think.

'Whoa! Is there something going on between you two that I should know about?' Georgia asked, intrigued as to why Abby had objected so strongly. 'That friendship story you keep spinning is wearing a bit thin.'

'And yet it's true,' Abby said, her voice now calm and controlled. 'What I meant was, he's not going to have a lot of time for socialising. He's here specifically to work on his new book.'

She did feel a tiny bit guilty for not being totally honest

with her friend, but she was well aware of Georgia's inability to keep a secret. And the way Abby was feeling about Daniel was something she definitely did not want becoming common knowledge.

'Don't you think it's about time we met him?' Ellie asked.

'I'll see what I can do,' Abby said, unwilling to commit Daniel to anything without speaking to him first.

'Sounds to me like someone wants to keep him all to herself,' Georgia said, still not entirely convinced by Abby's assertion that there was nothing going on.

'Well, if you had a gorgeous guy sleeping naked in your spare room, I'm pretty sure you wouldn't want to share him either,' Abby said, joining in with her friends' laughter, finding humour to be the best way of handling her complicated emotions.

NINE

Abby arrived home in a taxi just after one-thirty. Asha and Ellie had gone home at eleven, leaving herself and Georgia, the two single ladies of the group, to move on to a club.

Abby's heart wasn't really in it. Her primary reason for going had been to keep Georgia company. She enjoyed the dancing, but wasn't in the mood for small talk and had no interest in pursuing any romantic possibilities. So when Georgia hooked up with her part-time boyfriend, Liam, Abby said her goodbyes and left early.

There was no alarm set for Sunday mornings, but Abby was on the balcony with her coffee before half-past eight. Daniel had told her his parents had invited him to go with them to some prior engagement at the golf club. He was unlikely to be back until the evening. Today would be the perfect time for one of her stress-free pyjama Sundays.

She settled down in front of the TV to watch the first two episodes of the latest Scandi crime drama that had caught her attention.

Next on the agenda was a relaxing soak in her own private spa bath for thirty minutes of pure bliss. She closed her eyes and centred her mind on nothing but the soothing sound of the bubbles, until the unwelcome but inevitable moment of the automatic switch-off told her it was time to get out. She wrapped herself up in her fluffy pink dressing gown and curled up with a book in her snuggle chair.

Twenty minutes later, the sound of someone knocking on the front door broke into the peaceful silence. Annoyed by the disturbance, she made her way downstairs to investigate. Looking through the peephole she was amazed to see Daniel standing there. Her annoyance instantly evaporated at the sight of him.

'You're always early,' she laughed, opening the door for him. 'What happened this time?'

'I thought I'd give the golf club a miss. There's a limit to the number of times I can take being introduced as "my son, Daniel, the famous author". Anyway, I'd rather be with you.' He gave her a quick kiss on the cheek as she shut the door behind him. 'Although it looks like I may have interrupted something,' he added, raising his eyebrows at Abby standing there in her dressing gown.

'Only me and a good book. That's all.'

'Great, because I was hoping we could go for a walk. I need to stretch my legs and breathe in some fresh air after that car journey.'

'I'd love to. Just let me go and get dressed.' She turned to him as she started up the stairs. 'Come up if you like. You can talk to me while I'm getting ready.'

More than happy to accept the invitation, he put down his bag, kicked off his shoes and followed her up the stairs.

'Who let you in?' she asked.

'The couple we met in the lift on Friday. They were on their way out. I was about to call you since you didn't answer the buzzer.'

'Sorry, I didn't hear it. I'd better give you your own set of keys.' She took the spare keys from her bedside drawer and handed them to him. 'They'll get you into the gym as well if you want to use that.'

'Thanks.' He sat down on the chair Abby had recently vacated, swivelling it round so that he was facing her. 'Not one of mine then,' he said, picking up the book she had left on the side table.

'I am allowed to read books by other authors.'

'Obviously, but this one's a bit lightweight.'

'And what's wrong with that? It's perfect reading for a lazy Sunday.'

She selected a few items of clothing from her walk-in wardrobe, then took them through to the bathroom, leaving the door ajar. 'How was golf with your dad yesterday?' she asked.

'It was good. He's definitely mellowed a bit. There was no constant fault-finding with my technique like there used to be.'

'And did you find anything else to talk about?'

'He told me how much he enjoyed *Patiently Humming*. That was a major surprise. It's the first time he's mentioned reading one of my books. I know I'll never get an apology for his vitriolic rant over my career choice, but at least he can finally appreciate my work.'

The bathroom door opened wider, and Abby stepped out. 'I'm so relieved the relationship between you is improving,' she said.

She was dressed in nothing but a T-shirt and her underwear, which grabbed Daniel's attention. 'Now that's a good look,' he said, winking at her and grinning broadly.

'Will you stop it!' But her eyes were smiling. He knew she didn't really object.

'What did you get up to last night?' he asked as she disappeared back into her wardrobe to pull on her leggings.

'We met for drinks and a meal at Duke's, then Asha and Ellie said goodnight, and Georgia and I went dancing.'

'You had a good time?'

'Yes, I did.' There were no more questions, so she didn't elaborate. She grabbed a pair of socks and came back out. 'I told the girls about your surprise arrival. Ellie and Georgia are dying to meet you.'

Daniel moved over to make room for her on the chair. 'Then I'll invite them to my party,' he said.

'Really? They would love that. Thanks.'

'My pleasure.'

'Do you like the colours up here?' Abby asked as she put on her socks. 'I wanted upstairs to have its own distinctive look.' In a complete change from the shades of aqua and beige that she had chosen for the downstairs rooms, upstairs there was a colour scheme of midnight blue and shades of purple.

'I like the disconnection with the rest of the flat,' he

said. 'You come up the stairs and into a unique space. I think you made a good decision.'

His arm lay across the back of the chair, and his fingers began playing with Abby's chestnut-brown hair that fell in soft waves below her shoulders. 'Although I'm pretty sure no guy lucky enough to be invited up to your personal sanctuary will be wasting time critiquing the décor,' he added with a smile.

'I wasn't asking for your opinion on that,' she said indignantly.

He let go of her hair and lightly stroked her face, feeling the soft warmth of her cheek on the back of his hand. 'I've made you blush again.'

'No you haven't,' she said, brushing his hand away. 'Sex is hardly a taboo subject between us.'

'Okay, so tell me what happened with the guy who took you out to dinner last week.'

Her thoughts returned to the previous Sunday, and the rather dull evening spent with a solicitor she had met through work. 'I enjoyed the meal, but nothing happened in the way you mean.'

'He didn't get an invite?'

'No. He's a nice enough guy, but for me there was no spark.'

'Not like there was between us.'

'That can easily be explained by science,' she said primly.

'I agree. It was science. Or if we want to be more specific, chemistry.'

It was obvious where he was going with this, but she refused to play along. 'We're best friends, of course there's chemistry between us.'

'I'm not talking about friendship. Have you never thought about us getting together?'

And there it was. She could hardly ignore it now. 'I may have done,' she said, shifting her position so she was sitting at an angle to him, bringing her knees up to her chest and hugging them tightly.

He knew exactly what she was doing. Whether consciously or not, she was shielding herself from him and from temptation.

'But we both know it can never happen,' she added.

'We do? And why's that?'

'Because it would ruin our friendship. Your friendship is the most important thing in the world to me, Daniel. I can't lose it. I can't lose you.'

'You'll never lose me. You know that.'

'What I know is that relationships break up all the time. We've both experienced that shift from sharing every single intimacy with someone to becoming practically strangers. I don't want that with you. I couldn't bear it. What we have now is forever. Let's not spoil it.'

He moved closer to her, his arms resting on top of her clutched knees, his forehead almost touching hers.

She felt her body tense, unsure of what he was going to do next. Would he kiss her? How would she react if he did?

'You know I love you,' he whispered, his gaze

threatening to melt her heart as she fought to keep her composure. Then, without warning, his face broke into a smile. 'But sometimes you can be far too sensible.'

Her body relaxed, and she returned his smile. He was back to being her best friend, that was something she *could* handle. 'Well, one of us has to be,' she said, standing up and pulling him to his feet. 'Now let's go and enjoy some of that fresh air you said you were in need of.'

TEN

They took a circular walk by the river. A popular route for runners and dog walkers, as well as family groups enjoying a Sunday afternoon stroll. Sometimes they smiled and said hello as they crossed paths with others, but they didn't interact any more than that.

Several of the passers-by would have been familiar with Daniel's novels. But in England he was a well-known author without being a well-known face, and that was exactly how he wanted it when he was with Abby.

After about twenty minutes, they crossed over a footbridge and walked back along the other side. 'Shall we sit for a bit?' Abby suggested as they approached an avenue of plane trees, interspersed with wooden benches.

'Why not?' Daniel said, stopping at the first unoccupied bench they came to.

'No, not this one.' She took his hand and walked to another bench a little further along. 'This one. It's Dad's bench.'

He read the small plaque engraved with Adam's full name, and the years of his birth and death. Underneath were the words: *Always in our Hearts*. 'Abby, I didn't know about this.'

'It took so long to arrange; it's only been here since July. I thought I'd wait until I could show you in person.'

They sat down together, enjoying the picturesque views across the river. 'It's a beautiful spot,' Daniel said. 'We're lucky no-one was sitting here already.'

'Oh, don't. It's still so new to me. I'm afraid I get upset if I find someone else using it. Is that awful?'

'No, it's understandable.' His arm went across her shoulders, and she rested her head against him. 'But it will get easier,' he added. 'And it's better if the bench is used, isn't it? Adam would love that.'

'You're right. He would.'

'I have so many happy memories of your dad, especially when we were young. I loved helping him in the garden. Plus all those days out during the school holidays. We had some fantastic times.'

'Yes, we did.' She sat up and took out her phone. 'Take a look at this photo that Mum scanned for me. I'm having it turned into a canvas picture to hang in the hall.' It was a panoramic view of a large sandy beach, deserted apart from a man and a young boy on the shoreline in the distance, flying a kite. 'Do you remember this?' she asked.

'I certainly do. Beth took some amazing photos. Kite-flying with your dad, that was a brilliant day out.'

'Apart from the wind blowing off the North Sea. That was a bit harsh.'

'What do you mean a bit harsh?' he laughed. 'It was perfect kite-flying weather.'

'I suppose it was, but not so good to sit in. Mum and I were huddled under blankets against the sea wall when she took the photo.'

'That must have been the day we had hot chocolate in that little café to warm you up.'

Abby smiled at the memory. 'Yes, it was.'

'And the walks we did across London, ticking off the boxes in your *I-Spy* book. Remember those?'

'I do. I loved those walks.' She rested her head against him once again. 'It feels so good to be sitting on Dad's bench with you and reminiscing like this. I miss those carefree days.'

'They were pretty special.'

He was silent for a moment, his mind searching for two appropriate words. Then he found what he was looking for: 'Gallivanting Generations.'

'That's exactly what we were. I like that.'

It didn't take her long to come up with her own two words. 'Happy Hearts.'

'And is your heart happy?'

'Yes. Very happy.'

'Good. Mine too,' he said, kissing her lightly on top of her head.

The cosy domestic routine that Abby had been wishing for began to fall into place over the next few days. They would have breakfast together before taking the fifteen minute walk to her office. Daniel would then return to the flat and spend several hours on his book.

Their alphabet game had come to a halt now that Daniel was concentrating full-time on his writing. Abby chose not to mention it. There would be plenty of time for a restart once his writing weeks were over.

He was true to his word and never objected to the interruption when she came home from work. And he would always take time to join her for dinner. She enjoyed having someone there to chat about the day.

Since the breakdown of her marriage, Abby had always lived by herself. Now and again guys had stayed over, but had never been given the opportunity to move in. She was not interested in I-love-yous or any long-term commitment. If they asked too much of her, it was time to say goodbye.

Her relationship with Daniel was different because they loved each other as friends. She had convinced herself there was nothing more to it than that. She was certainly not *in* love with him. In Abby's world, falling in love was full of risks. Only friendship was forever.

ELEVEN

On Thursday, Daniel took a midday break from writing and made another unexpected appearance at the office. He brought with him an indoor picnic of sandwiches, spinach salad and cheesecake.

Emily was delighted to see him, and continued the charade by buzzing through to Abby with the news that Francis Weston had arrived for another appointment.

'I have another surprise for you,' Daniel said when they had finished their lunch.

'Another one?' Abby laughed. 'What are you up to now?'

'I'm coming to pick you up tomorrow, so make sure you're ready to leave on time.'

'And?' she asked, eager to know what else he had in store for her.

He took out his phone. 'I've booked a weekend away for us at this place,' he said, showing her a picture of the nearby spa.

'Brook Grange? Daniel, that's wonderful.' She gave him a hug. 'When did you arrange this?'

'Last weekend. I wanted to make sure we spent this weekend together.'

She listened to his commentary as he scrolled through photos on the website. 'We have two adjoining rooms with patios. We can eat there or in the restaurant, whatever you prefer. I've booked massages for both of us. Anything else is entirely up to you. You know the sort of thing they have.'

'Thank you so much, Daniel. You're too good to me.'

'Nonsense. It's my thanks to you for taking it all in your stride when I turned up like I did.'

'I love your surprises. No-one else does surprises like you do.'

It was impossible to stop word getting around that Daniel was in the building once again. Some of Abby's colleagues made excuses to linger in reception at the end of their lunch break, ambushing Daniel before Abby could show him out. But he was happy to stop for a few selfies.

He also signed a copy of *Patiently Humming* for Helena, who had been carrying the book in her handbag all week on the off chance that Daniel would make a return visit.

On Friday he was back, but this time he waited outside for Abby. Within the hour they were checking in at Brook Grange. Half an hour after that they were unwinding in the hot tub.

The weekend went exactly as they had hoped. Plenty of time to relax and enjoy each other's company. Clients and deadlines, along with the usual stresses of everyday life, were all but forgotten for two and a half glorious days.

Abby felt rejuvenated after their spa weekend, but for

Daniel it had the opposite effect. He found it hard to get back into his natural flow. His ideas had stalled. His mind clogged up with too many disjointed thoughts.

He spent most of Monday walking down by the river, hoping the fresh air and the surroundings would clear his head and help bring the inspiration he needed. It worked to some extent, and on Tuesday he began to expand on the notes he had made.

When Abby came home from work on Wednesday, she found Daniel sprawled on the floor, papers everywhere. 'Right on cue,' he said as she appeared from the hall. 'Can you help me with a sex scene?'

'Excuse me?' she said, giggling nervously. She had not been expecting that as soon as she walked in. 'Is this one of your famous chat-up lines?'

'My best one,' he grinned. 'Works every time.'

'Well, I think I need an explanation. And before that, a little hello would be nice.'

'Sorry.' He stood up and walked over to her, taking her in his arms and kissing her on the cheek. 'Hello, Abby,' he said solemnly. 'How was your day?'

'It went very well, thank you. How about you?'

'It was all going very nicely until I found I needed some help.'

'With sex?'

'Indeed.'

She sat down and spun another stool round for him. 'Go on then. Explain.'

'I'm writing a scenario where the two detectives end up

having sex, but it needs to be spontaneous. I have this idea that they're sorting through paperwork on the floor, and somehow get themselves into a compromising position. I want to see if it's feasible.'

'And that's where I come in?'

'That's where you come in.'

'So you want me to believe that from your vast experience on the subject you don't already have an incident that fits the scene perfectly?'

'Ouch!' he laughed. 'Thanks for that assault on my character.'

'Well?' she insisted.

'Yes, I want you to believe it. Because I don't. I really don't.'

'I thought spontaneous was your middle name.'

'And I thought you liked being involved with my writing.'

'I do. I'm just wondering what your motives are.'

He smiled at her, then said slowly, 'Indecent Intentions.'

So they were back to their game. 'Do you have all these stored in your head?' she laughed.

But Daniel didn't laugh. 'What do you have stored in *your* head?' he asked softly. His eyes were watching her carefully, his expression giving nothing away.

She put all her concentration into the game, doing her best to ignore Daniel's odd behaviour. Jam, jelly, jolly, jump, ran through her head and were immediately rejected. 'It's so unfair. The letters are much harder on my side of the alphabet.'

'Rubbish. There are plenty of J's to choose from.'

Of course, it didn't really matter what she said. There were no strict rules apart from the initial letters. But she wanted to give it meaning. How did Daniel make her feel? Confused. Sometimes anxious. But mostly he made her happy. The words were suddenly obvious: 'Just Joy.'

'There you go. Perfect. Now, will you help me or not? Honestly, there's no hidden agenda.' He paused, then added, 'Unless you're into method acting. I'd be happy to go along with that.'

'*You* are impossible,' she said, relieved that he was back in a flirtatious mood. She jumped off the stool and opened the fridge. 'I'd better start dinner.'

He came up behind her, reaching over her shoulder to push the door shut. 'I promise I'll be good,' he said, his tone still playful.

She gave a sigh and turned round. 'Fine. I'll go and get changed.'

'You mean you'll do it?'

'Yes, I'll do it.' If she was honest, there was never going to be any other outcome. But it had done Daniel no harm to wait for an answer.

'There's no need to change,' he said. 'That dress is great.'

'Wouldn't she be wearing trousers?'

'No. She's not on duty. She had to cut short a date. But go and change if you want.'

'Let's just get on with it.'

He gave a mock salute. 'Yes Ma'am.'

'So now I'm bossy?'

'When have you not been?' he laughed. 'I'm used to it. That's why I'll be the ideal husband for you.'

She chose to ignore his comment this time. But if it kept happening, she knew she would have to say something. Surely he would understand if she made it clear to him that it was making her feel uncomfortable?

They both sat on the floor, then Daniel laid down on his front. 'Right, you start to stretch over me to reach one of the papers, then I turn onto my back and you end up on top of me and in my arms.'

She followed his direction to the letter. But instead of landing on top of him, as he rolled over his body pushed her onto the floor beside him. 'Oh dear,' she giggled. 'You may want to try a different approach.'

He wasn't deterred. 'No, it could work if I'm lying on my side instead. We'll try again.'

On the second attempt he put one arm around her as he turned, and this time she stayed on top of him. His hands moved onto her hips. He smiled up at her, his eyes teasing. 'Has anyone ever told you how great it feels having you on top?'

'Many times,' she said, smiling back. 'Is that part of the dialogue?'

'It could be.'

But she couldn't sustain the flirty vibes for much longer if she stayed in the same position. Her emotions were threatening to take over. She rolled onto the floor and lay down on her back next to him. A much safer place.

'So what happens with these two?' she asked. 'Is it just

a one-off or do they have a relationship?'

'They give it a go, but one of them is keeping secrets.'

'Which one? And what sort of secrets?'

'You know you can read what I've written whenever you want.'

'Thanks. Maybe I'll take a look after dinner. And just ask if you need help with anything else.'

He grinned broadly. 'I can tell it's going to be great fun being married to you.'

She gave a loud sigh. It was definitely time to confront him on the issue. 'Daniel, please stop bringing up our marriage pact.'

'But I always keep my promises to you. Why should this one be any different?'

'Because I'm not eight years old anymore. I'd rather keep my best friend than lose another husband.'

'And I thought you loved me.'

'I do love you, but that doesn't mean I'm going to marry you.' She leant over him. 'So. Stop. Bringing. It. Up,' she said, jabbing him in the chest to emphasise her words.

'Ow! You could do a lot of damage with that finger.' He lifted up his T-shirt and rubbed his chest.

She kissed the offending finger, and placed it gently over the red mark it had left. 'Is that better?'

'Much better.'

'But did you hear what I said?'

'I heard every word.'

'Good,' she said, lying down beside him once again.

They lay quietly together for a few moments until

Daniel broke the silence. 'I see Beth still has your bridesmaid photo in pride of place.'

'I know. It was one of Dad's favourites. I think she has the dress itself somewhere in the loft.'

'At least you finally managed to take it off. You were hardly out of it that summer.'

'I loved that dress. I thought of it as my very own wedding dress. There are even photos of me wearing it on the beach. It was so special, there was no way I was only going to wear it once.'

'And you're adamant you'll never have a third one? Or is it just me you're refusing to marry?'

'Daniel, you're not even trying. Marriage is a serious business. I don't like you teasing me about it.'

'I'm sorry, Abby. I had no idea it was upsetting you. I won't mention our pact again.'

'Thank you.' Now that was settled, there was something she was ready to confess. 'Actually, I do have a little secret about marriage that you might like to hear.'

'Don't tell me you and Gavin never divorced,' he laughed.

'No, that definitely happened. I wouldn't get something like that wrong.'

He propped himself up on his elbow so he could see her face. 'Go on then, tell me the secret.'

'Well, I've had this idea that once I've stopped work, and if we're both still single, we could travel the world together. You and me. And then, who knows? Maybe I'll be ready to honour our pact.'

He rolled onto his back, groaning theatrically. 'You're asking me to wait another thirty-five years? That's asking too much.'

'You don't think I'm worth it?'

The flirty banter between them came to a sudden stop as his ever-changing mood turned back to serious. 'Beth asked me when I was going to settle down.'

'Really? She never mentioned that to me. What did you say?'

'When the right woman agrees to have me.'

Abby was surprised at this response. Daniel had always said he wasn't ready to settle down. 'So you think Ms Right is out there somewhere, do you?' she asked, keeping her voice light.

'Why not? Even those of us who aren't looking can suddenly feel that tug on our heart strings.'

'Well, whoever she is, she'll be very lucky to have you,' she said, snuggling up against him.

He put his arm around her, his mind elsewhere. There was so much more he wanted to tell her, but he couldn't be certain how she would react. The time would have to be right. The words carefully chosen. He wasn't ready.

In the silence, a tiny little seed began to sprout in Abby's mind. But she squashed it down, refusing to acknowledge its significance.

TWELVE

It was a more subdued Daniel who joined Abby for breakfast the next morning. She knew he was having issues with his writing. After reading through what he had already written, she found it very atmospheric and exciting. But what Daniel was concerned about was the quantity. He was still a long way from reaching the target he had set himself for the three weeks.

The night before he had told her he was considering going back to the hotel for a few days.

'Have you come to a decision?' she asked as he sat down beside her.

'I have. I've booked myself a cottage in the Lake District. It looks the perfect place for spending time alone. I'll be able to focus and get back on track.'

This news bore no comparison to what Abby had been expecting. The Lake District? He may as well have said Lake Como. They wouldn't be meeting up at all. It was a clean break.

'I hope I haven't driven you away.'

'Not exactly. You've been brilliant, Abby. But you are a distraction.'

'And I tried so hard not to be.'

'I know, and I appreciate that. It'll just be for a few days. I'll be leaving early tomorrow and back Tuesday evening. I'm not hiring another car; I'll go by train. I've booked a taxi to take me to the cottage.'

'I can drop you off at the station and be there to pick you up.'

'That would be great. Thanks. And I'd like to take you to Luca's this evening. What do you think?'

'I think that's a lovely idea, although you'll be lucky to get in at this late stage.'

'So I discovered last night. I've made a booking for six o'clock, it was all they had. I thought I could pick you up from work, then we'll go straight there. Or I could try somewhere else?'

'No, six o'clock will be fine. And will you be needing any shopping?'

'It's all sorted. I've arranged for them to leave a box of essentials for me when I arrive.'

'You've got it all planned, haven't you?' There was a touch of bitterness to her voice that she never intended. 'I'm sorry, Daniel. That wasn't meant to sound unkind.'

'You do understand why I'm going, don't you?' he asked, taking her hand in his.

'Of course I do. You've made the right decision. It was always going to be harder to write when you're living with someone else.'

'Abby, I've loved being here with you. I've never regretted coming. Please don't think that.'

'Well, I won't now,' she said, giving him a smile.

As they made their way into town, Daniel was a lot quieter than usual, resisting Abby's attempts to engage him in conversation. He only gave mumbled replies, making it obvious that he wasn't really listening.

She soon gave up trying, although she was anxious to know what was troubling him. Maybe they could talk about it this evening. Or maybe it would be left until after he came back. Whatever it was, she felt sure he would tell her eventually.

'So you'll be here just before six?' she asked as they walked round the final corner.

'I'll be here.'

They stopped in their usual place to say goodbye, and Daniel finally gave her his attention. 'I'm sorry I've been ignoring you,' he said, wrapping his arms around her. 'I've had a lot on my mind.'

'It's okay. You did warn me things might get difficult. Just as long as you're all right.'

'Don't worry about me. I'll be fine.' His forced smile had a profound sadness to it. Telling her not to worry was like telling her not to breathe.

'I'll see you later,' she said, her smile so much warmer than his. 'Take care.'

'You too. Have a good day.' But he made no move to leave. His fingers gently touched her arm, his eyes holding her interest. Once again she had a feeling that he was going to confide in her, but then he pulled away with a sigh. 'I'd better go.'

He turned and left her standing on the footpath, where she stayed until he vanished round the corner. Out of sight but never out of her thoughts. As soon as she crossed the threshold, she pushed her work schedule to the front of her mind. But Daniel remained, and in quieter moments he would take centre stage once again.

When Abby stepped outside at ten to six, Daniel was there waiting for her. His appearance was completely different from that morning: he wore a jacket over a dark T-shirt; his jeans and trainers had been replaced by smart trousers and shoes; he was clean-shaven and his hair neatly styled.

'Wow, you look amazing,' she said as he came towards her. 'You've scrubbed up really well.'

'Thanks. I didn't want you walking in on the arm of a slob.'

'That would never happen; you always look good. But I do appreciate the extra effort.'

They took the short walk to Luca's. Abby introduced Daniel to Gina, who was at the front desk this time.

'So where's the charming Marco tonight?' Daniel asked as he read through the menu.

'I've no idea. You're not jealous of him, are you?' she teased.

He looked surprised by her suggestion. 'Why would I be? Because he knows you more intimately than I do?'

How could she have said something so stupid? She made a clumsy attempt to explain. 'I was just reminded of what Ellie said when I told the girls I'd taken you to Luca's the day you arrived. She asked if I'd done it to make you jealous.'

'And had you?'

'Of course not. I don't think like that.'

'I know you don't. And you know that I'm not the jealous type.'

'I do. I'm sorry. Can we start this conversation again?'

'Actually, I'd like to answer your question.'

'Okay,' she said, a little nervously.

'No, I'm not jealous. I'm not jealous of any of the guys you've known. Their part in your life is just fleeting, whereas I will always be a part of it.'

'Always,' she said with a smile.

But he didn't return her smile. He held her gaze for a few seconds, then his eyes returned to the menu.

He was all smiles for the waitress, Chloe, when she took their order. Abby felt uncomfortable and embarrassed at his behaviour. She was used to Daniel's flirting, and it had never been a problem for her. What she wasn't used to was the feeling that she was somehow being excluded.

For one horrified moment she thought she was going to cry. She stayed where she was until Chloe had left their table, then she couldn't hold her composure any longer. 'Excuse me,' she muttered to Daniel, avoiding eye contact as she stood up and headed for the ladies.

She dabbed at her eyes with a tissue before any tears fell. But now she was feeling hot and flustered. Definitely not ready to go back to the table. She took off her jacket, had a drink of cold water, then sat down on a chair. Someone came in, looked at her oddly, and asked if she was okay.

'I'm fine, thank you. Just cooling down.'

'Yes, it is rather warm in the restaurant,' the woman said.

But Abby knew she couldn't hide forever. It was time to go back. She was surprised to find Daniel waiting for her in the corridor. 'Sorry. Have I been ages?'

'No, *I'm* sorry. I've got far too much running through my mind right now, and I've been taking my frustration out on you. Can you forgive me?'

'Of course. But please don't shut me out, Daniel. Talk to me. I'm always here for you.'

'I know. I don't deserve you.'

She took hold of his hand. 'I'm afraid you're stuck with me,' she smiled. 'Now, are you ready to eat?'

'I certainly am. I haven't eaten since breakfast.'

Chloe arrived with their sharing platter as soon as they sat down. 'Is everything okay?' she asked.

'Yes, everything's fine,' Daniel said. 'Thanks for waiting.'

'No problem. Enjoy your meal.' And she left them to it.

'Did you manage to get any writing done today?' Abby asked as she spread aubergine and peppers on her ciabatta.

'The morning was good. Then Paula phoned in the afternoon, and I gave up after that. She's not helping with my stress levels.'

'Did you tell her you were going away for a few days?'

'I did. I also told her I'd be switching off my phone.'

'She could hardly object to that.'

'No.' He gave her a smile, his body visibly more relaxed.

'That's better,' she said, relieved to see him smiling again. 'Are you ready to talk to me?'

'I'm finding it frustrating that I'm not as far ahead with my writing as I'd hoped,' he said. 'A few days away, and I'll be fine. Honestly.'

She left it at that. The last thing Daniel needed was to sit through twenty questions. That would only add to his stress.

But she couldn't shake off the feeling that there was something more. A strong feeling that he was still shutting her out.

THIRTEEN

The following morning, Abby drove Daniel to the railway station to catch the six fifteen train.

'You'll let me know when you get there, won't you?' she asked as they stopped at the ticket barriers.

'I'll text you.'

'I hope it goes well, Daniel.'

'Thanks. I'm confident it will.'

'And when you get back we can start to focus on your birthday and our busy weekend.'

'Absolutely.' He gave her a hug before making his way through the barrier. Sensing that she was still watching him, he turned round when he reached the steps and raised his hand in goodbye.

With her head down and her steps heavy, she made her way back to the car park and waited by the metal fence. Looking down at the platforms below, it was easy to pick out Daniel standing at the far end of platform four. A solitary figure in a navy padded jacket, his hair blowing in the breeze.

As the train arrived he was swallowed up by the sudden onrush of people, but she didn't move from her spot. She watched as the train pulled away, and continued watching until it had disappeared from her sight.

Abby was at her desk when the text from Daniel came through: *Journey smooth and uneventful. Cottage just what I need. Views spectacular. Relaxed and ready to write. Thanks for everything. D xx*

It brought a smile to her face, but she knew better than to reply. He would not expect her to, or even want her to, and she respected that.

Her holiday leave had been put back a day now that Daniel wouldn't be here until the evening of the twentieth. Then she would be starting her three week break, although she would try and go in for an hour or two each week to make sure there weren't too many surprises waiting for her when she officially returned.

At the end of her day at the office she wasn't ready to go home to an empty flat. Instead, she took a stroll along the river to Adam's bench. The bench and Adam's garden were the two places where she felt closest to him. Where she liked to sit alone in quiet reflection.

Perhaps because there had been so much talk about it lately, her mind went back to the time when she had announced that Daniel was going to be her husband. It was just a few days after Holly's wedding, and Abby had been wearing her bridesmaid dress.

Adam had been there and heard it all. She remembered him lifting her onto his lap and telling her he would be the proudest father in the world when he walked her down the aisle at her wedding, whether it was Daniel or someone else waiting for her.

'Daddy, of course it will be Daniel,' she had giggled. 'But I don't want a car like Aunty Holly. I want a carriage and white horses. Can I?'

He had smiled affectionately at her and given her a big hug. 'I'll see what I can do.' But there are some dreams that will never be. She still lived with the guilt that he had been denied his dream of walking her down the aisle.

Her actual wedding had borne no resemblance to the one she had dreamt of as a little girl. No white horses. No dancing under the stars. And definitely no big sparkly dress. The most suitable outfit she'd packed had been a cream and black silk dress, which she accessorised with a pair of strappy black sandals. She had been pleased with her appearance, and so had Gavin, but there was nothing particularly bridal about it. Not even a bouquet. But she hadn't cared at all. She was in love.

Daniel had been the first person Abby had told about the wedding, sending him a text that same day: *Getting married this afternoon! Since we're in Vegas, why not?*

She had been expecting some witty response involving Elvis or white suits, but he had surprised her with his reply: *Are you happy?*

Of course! We're madly in love and blissfully happy x

Then that's all that matters. Congratulations x

The hastily organised reception by her husband's parents back home in England was the only occasion when her three favourite men had been in the same place at the same time: Adam, her father; Daniel, her childhood friend; and Gavin, the one she had pledged herself to for the rest of her life.

Daniel had been travelling round Canada on a work visa, but had wanted to be there for Abby. He flew back the day before the reception.

On their wedding day, Abby and Gavin had been together for twenty wonderful months. But when the initial honeymoon glow had begun to wear off, when the student life they had shared was replaced by the monotony of everyday domestic life, the cracks had begun to show.

Their conflicting work schedules had eventually led to separate social lives. From that point on it was inevitable that their marriage wouldn't last.

She could still remember with perfect clarity the precise moment when she had known they had no future. Just an ordinary Sunday morning, three months after their first anniversary, when suddenly she'd heard the front door shutting. Gavin had gone out with no goodbye. No explanation. Nothing.

Less than half an hour later he had returned as calmly as he had left, a pint of milk in his hand. 'Why didn't you say you were going out?' she asked. Not accusing, just puzzled.

He had looked surprised at her question. 'Sorry, did you need me for something?'

She had shrugged her shoulders. 'No. I just wondered why you left without saying a word.'

They had stared at one another for a few seconds, both

realising it was the beginning of the end. Both accepting that the love was starting to fade.

Within a month their flat was up for sale, and Gavin had moved out. And he had moved on rather quicker than Abby, spending that Christmas skiing in the French Alps with his temporary new lover. It would be the following summer before Abby began another relationship. The first of several short-lived romances in the years after the end of her marriage.

By this time Daniel had settled in Toronto, and Abby spent that Christmas with him. He was there for a hug when she needed one, but there were no more tears. They broke with tradition, having poutine for Christmas dinner followed by butter tarts. New Year's Eve had been spent watching the fireworks, their lips meeting for a friendly New Year's Eve kiss.

Daniel was the perfect antidote. Apart from the minutes spent in her lonely bed each night, before finally falling into a welcome sleep, Gavin had barely entered her thoughts.

Like their wedding, their divorce had been a mutual decision. No bitterness or animosity. And neither one of them in a hurry to try marriage again. It was in the days before the quickie divorce and another two years had passed before it became official. They had celebrated the occasion with a bottle of expensive champagne and one last night together. A very pleasant – but very final – goodbye.

It was not the celebration Abby would expect many of

her clients to indulge in. The couples she saw were at the other end of the breakup spectrum. The ones where love had turned into loathing, desire into disgust. For them it was all about recriminations and playing the blame game. She was grateful that her own marriage hadn't descended to that level, yet the fact that their union had been such a colossal failure had hurt her deeply.

It was still hard to accept that she had allowed herself to make such a mistake by letting her emotions overrule her logical thinking. And it was because of this uncharacteristic mistake that she remained adamant the door would stay firmly shut on any idea of a repeat performance.

As she sat alone with her thoughts, she was suddenly awoken from her reminiscing by the sharp coldness of the evening breeze touching her cheeks. It was time to make her way home.

After dinner Abby curled up on the sofa with a cup of tea. But her mind refused to relax, her thoughts constantly returning to Daniel. She couldn't let go of the feeling that he was keeping something from her. There had been times in the past when he had delayed telling her something until he could find the right moment. His decision to move to Canada was one such occasion.

The Daniel that he showed to the outside world was talented, charismatic and generous. To his friends he was also loyal, thoughtful and kind. Abby could only think of one reason why he would withhold information from her: he was worried about how she would react. So he was waiting for the right setting, searching for the right words, to minimise any hurt she might feel.

All those times when she thought he had been trying to tell her something. On their way to the restaurant after his surprise arrival. When she had found him in the kitchen on that first night. Right up to when he had walked her to work the day before he left for the Lake District. So many times.

And all those times when he had been affectionate and flirty with her? That was just Daniel. She could never take him seriously. But had he been trying to reassure her that nothing had changed between them before unveiling his secret?

As she thought through the possibilities in her mind, the seed that had been planted in her head began to grow until it had pushed itself into her consciousness. Once there, she could no longer push it back.

She had never even considered that she would find the man of her dreams after the end of her marriage. She enjoyed dating, had met some great guys amongst the not so great ones, but she had no interest in commitment. She knew only too well how fragile that could be.

But what about Daniel's dreams? What if that beautiful, charming, independent woman she had imagined as his ideal partner was no longer in her imagination? What if he had actually met her?

Now she was convinced that was the answer. What other explanation could there be? He must have found someone he wanted to share the rest of his life with. The signs were everywhere. Hadn't he talked about taking a chance and ending up somewhere amazing? About how anyone could feel a sudden tug on their heart strings? Then there was his unexpected answer to Beth's question. It all pointed in the same direction.

How could she not be happy for him? She was his best friend; of course she wanted him to be happy. But wouldn't it change everything between them? Was it conceivable that another woman could accept the deep connection they shared? Would agree to their regular lengthy video calls?

The thought of where it might lead was hard for her to handle. How could she possibly let him go?

Her suggestion to Daniel that they get together later in life hadn't been an entirely new idea. She had often thought how wonderful it would be for them to spend those years travelling round the world together. Then stopping off on some exotic island and finally getting married.

She had never really thought of it as a serious dream, more of a delightful fantasy. Until now. Now, when it seemed there was no chance of it becoming a reality, she realised that to spend her final years with Daniel was what she wanted more than anything else.

FOURTEEN

Abby drove to her mother's house for lunch on Saturday: through the winding country roads where she knew every sharp bend and dip; up the steep hill that would be closed to traffic on the rare occasions when there was a downfall of heavy winter snow; through the small town with the primary school where Beth now taught; then down a longer, more gentle, slope which led to the village that had barely changed since Abby was a child.

'What have you done with Daniel?' was the first thing Beth asked when she opened the front door and saw Abby standing there alone.

'Oh, Mum. I'm sorry. I should have told you he wasn't coming. I completely forgot that you would be expecting him.'

'Don't worry, it's not a problem.' They hugged each other, then made their way into the kitchen and sat down at the table, which had been laid for three. 'What's happened?' Beth asked as she removed one of the place settings.

'Daniel has taken himself off to the Lake District so he can concentrate more on his book. Apparently, I'm too much of a distraction.'

'Oh dear! Does this mean it's been difficult having him to stay?'

'No, I can't say that. It's been great. We have breakfast together, then he walks me to work. I've got used to him being there when I come home, having dinner together, talking about how we've spent the day. Coming home to an empty flat last night felt really strange.'

It would have been the perfect opportunity for Abby to confide in Beth about her suspicions that Daniel had fallen in love. That he had found someone he was ready to commit to. The unknown Ms Right.

But it would be impossible for her to explain how she had reached this conclusion without revealing her true feelings to her mother. And she was not yet ready to do that.

In contrast, Abby had plenty of words to say about the subject to Asha when she dropped in to see her on her way home. Rakesh was not going to be there, so Abby would be able to talk freely.

Asha listened carefully to what Abby had to say, but was sceptical about the assumptions she had made. 'To be honest, I think you've misread the situation. If he's met someone, surely he would have told you when he was in Canada? He can't have only just met her. I don't see what reason he would have to say nothing. It makes no sense.'

'It makes perfect sense,' Abby said, irritated with her friend for not agreeing with her analysis. 'He knows I'll be worried about how it will affect our own relationship, so he'll want to choose the right time to break it to me.'

'I would have thought as his best friend he would be excited to tell you. And he would expect you to be happy for him.'

'But what else could it be?'

Asha hesitated, then said carefully, 'He may be sick?'

This suggestion was immediately disregarded by Abby. 'No way. That is definitely something he would tell me. And I would have noticed the signs. It can't possibly be that.'

'Then it could be he's been stressed about his writing. When he comes back he'll be like his old self again.'

Abby refused to be swayed. 'What about the other things he said? They were nothing to do with his writing.'

'And nothing to suggest he was talking about his current situation, either.'

'So you think I'm being ridiculous?'

'I think you need to see it through your solicitor's eyes rather than through your emotions. There's absolutely no evidence for your theory.'

Abby gave a sigh, still not convinced. 'But I'm certain he's hiding something. And the only plausible explanation is that he's met his soul mate.'

She searched her mind for some concrete evidence. 'He's been here since the beginning of the month and not brought anyone back to the flat. Doesn't that say something?'

'Yes, it does. It says that he's here to spend time with

his best friend, not to meet other women. And even if he was interested, he would see it as disrespectful to you to bring some stranger back to your home for the night.'

This time Abby reluctantly found herself agreeing with what Asha was saying. Daniel wouldn't want to use her flat like that. Then again, he had the option to check back into the hotel and hadn't done that either. She still found it difficult to dismiss her well-thought-out theory, however hard Asha tried to persuade her she was wrong.

Asha saw the concern on Abby's face and made one more attempt to put her mind at ease. 'Don't worry about losing him, Abby. In the unlikely event that you're right and he has found someone, I can't see him being with anyone who wouldn't accept his best friend. You're part of the package.'

'Or the baggage.'

'No, don't say that!' But they both laughed, and Abby felt more relaxed.

The conversation moved on to arrangements for the following weekend. 'There'll be a break between the barbecue and the party,' Abby said. 'I think Olivia wants to make sure there won't be hours of continuous drinking.'

'You can't blame her. And it will give us time to go back to the hotel and get changed. I'm assuming it will be smart for the party?'

'There won't be any rules, but I'll be dressing up. And I've bought Daniel a shirt for his birthday that I'm hoping he'll be wearing.'

'No doubt Georgia will win the prize for the most

revealing outfit.'

'As long as she keeps her hands off Daniel.'

'Who knows? There could be an irresistible attraction between them.'

'Please don't say that!'

'At least it will prove he hasn't found his soul mate.'

'It's not funny, Asha.'

'Just think about it for a moment. Daniel has found his forever love, or Daniel has a short-lived fling with Georgia. Which would you prefer?'

'I'd prefer it if neither happened. But Daniel and Georgia together would be horrendous.'

Daniel finding his soul mate wasn't sounding quite so bad to Abby after all.

Lying in bed that night with her thoughts keeping her awake, Abby realised it was time to let go of her negative mood, and cherish what she had with Daniel whilst he was with her. Then be a good friend and support him in his decision. Be happy for him. It was the very least she could do.

And there was absolutely no reason to believe that a long-term girlfriend would mean the loss of his friendship; Asha had been right about that. She recalled Daniel's words to her when they were in Luca's the day before he left. Hadn't he told her he would always be in her life? Why was she doubting him and overthinking everything?

If she didn't start to change her perspective, she could be the one to end their relationship by driving him away with her paranoia. She would never forgive herself if it was through her own actions that she ended up losing her best friend.

FIFTEEN

On Tuesday evening, Abby was back at the railway station waiting for Daniel's return. It wasn't lost on her that the date was the twentieth – the original starting date of his visit. The day when she would have expected to be driving down to Heathrow to collect him. Instead it was only a fifteen-minute drive to the station.

Just a few minutes after his train appeared on the arrivals board, Daniel was through the barriers and walking towards her. Her face showed the joy she felt on seeing him again, but she kept her arms by her side and waited for Daniel to make the first move. 'Hey,' he said softly, kissing her on the cheek. 'I've missed you.'

'I've missed you too,' she said, slipping her arm through his. They made their way to the car surrounded by a crowd of fellow passengers on the same course. There were no further words between them until Abby had pulled out of the station car park. 'So how did it go?' she asked.

'It was good. I'm where I need to be, more or less. Although I still have to figure out that sex scene. I decided to scrap what I'd already written.'

'So our little enactment was just a waste of time, then?'

'I wouldn't say that. It meant I could rule out my first idea, so it wasn't entirely wasted. And it was a lot of fun testing it out, wasn't it?' he grinned. 'Do you think you could be up for another try?'

'I could be,' she said with a smile. 'But I thought you were taking a break from writing for now. At least until after your birthday.'

'I did say that, didn't I?' he said, noticeably more relaxed than he had been when he left. 'You're right. It can wait. But do you want to look at what I've done so far?'

'Yes, I'd love to.' She was impatient to read it.

Soon after arriving home they had settled on the sofa, Abby with Daniel's laptop balanced on her legs. She became so gripped by the developing story that she had no idea Daniel had fallen asleep beside her.

'I love it,' she said when she reached the end. 'I can't wait for the next instalment.' Getting no response, she turned to face him and saw what had happened. She put the laptop gently down on the coffee table, then said softly, 'It's bedtime, sleepyhead.'

He opened his eyes and gave a weary smile. 'Sorry, did I drift off? I only slept for a few hours' each night. I'm exhausted.' He let her help him to his feet, and within minutes he had swapped the convenience of the sofa for the comfort of his bed and a blissful sleep.

Daniel was still asleep when Abby came downstairs at eight the next morning. It reminded her of the first night he had spent there, when she had gone into his room as he slept and gently woken him up. But this time she would let him sleep for as long as he needed. She wouldn't be leaving for work today. There was no valid reason for her to go into his room. She made herself a coffee and took it outside. Breakfast could wait until Daniel was ready to join her.

Her thoughts turned to the upcoming party, and she began to think of it as an ending of sorts. A celebration not just of Daniel's birthday, but of all the years of their close friendship. Their undeniable connection and love for one another. After the party they would have their talk, and he would confirm her assumptions were correct. She would put on a brave face and be happy for him.

Perhaps he would promise her that nothing would change. Surely that would be a promise too hard to keep? It was inevitable that things would change. How could they not? They would keep in touch, but it could never be the same. Their video calls would become shorter and less frequent. She would no longer be the person he would automatically turn to when he needed to talk.

But he had given them this extra time together. She would always be grateful to him for that. Even when he had told her his secret, they would still have over two weeks before he left. Time to ask questions, time for his answers to put her mind at ease.

And when she went over to Toronto at Christmas, he would introduce her to Ms Right. How would she deal with that? Her imagination took on a life of its own, and she saw them becoming firm friends. If Daniel was in love with his Ms Right, wouldn't she learn to love her, too?

As Abby sat out on the balcony contemplating her future, it started to become clear to her what she should do. She should embrace the change. If Daniel was ready to begin a new life, couldn't she do the same? Who knew where she could be in a year's time if she put in the effort?

She remembered the couple's therapy course she had been considering. It would be so inspiring to help couples reconnect and overcome their difficulties. To help them reignite their love rather than only helping those who were at the end of their married life. The course would be starting in January, the perfect time for new starts. All sorts of opportunities would open up for her. She couldn't let the chance pass her by.

When Daniel walked into the kitchen an hour later, he found Abby at the island on her laptop. 'I trust that's not work,' he said.

'Not exactly. I thought I'd apply for that therapy course I've been thinking about.'

'That's a great idea.'

'I should hear in a couple of weeks if I've been accepted.'

He gave her a smile. 'You'll be fine.'

As they sat out on the balcony, enjoying breakfast together, Daniel unwittingly disrupted Abby's plans for his birthday surprise. 'I'm thinking of walking into town later,' he said. 'I need to find a shirt for Saturday night.'

'I'm not sure they'll have what you're looking for,' she said, wondering how she could put him off without making it too obvious.

'But it has to be worth a look.' He gave her a sideways glance. 'You don't sound too keen. Did you have plans for us today?'

'No, not really. Apart from a visit to the supermarket. I spoke to your mum while you were away. I'm going to be making some food to take down for lunch on Friday. Cheese palmiers, brownies, and a pasta salad. I need to pick up a few things.'

It was a hopeless attempt to take his mind off the shirt. She didn't really expect it to work, and she was right.

'Sounds good. And since neither one of us is working, we'll have plenty of time to do both.'

'Yes, we will,' she said, resigned to the fact that she would have to surprise him with the shirt today.

Whilst Daniel was at the gym, Abby went up to her bedroom to retrieve his present from her bottom drawer. In its box and already gift-wrapped.

She was checking her list for the supermarket when Daniel returned, his hair still damp from the shower.

'What do you want to do first?' he asked, sitting down beside her.

'First you can close your eyes. And don't move.'

'What are you up to?' he laughed, but did as she asked.

'You're not the only one who can do surprises.' She took his present out of the cupboard where she had hidden it and placed it in front of him. 'Happy birthday,' she said, kissing him on the cheek.

He opened his eyes. 'You want me to open it now?'

'I think you should.'

He tore off the paper and realised what had happened as soon as he saw the box. 'I put my foot in it, didn't I?'

'Just a bit.'

'Sorry, Abby. But this is great. Thank you so much.'

'You haven't even seen it yet! You might not like it.'

'That's highly unlikely. You've known me long enough to know what my tastes are.' He opened the lid and took out the long-sleeved soft cotton shirt, in an abstract print of greens and blues.

'It's fantastic. Thank you,' he said, standing up to give her a hug. He took off his T-shirt, undid the shirt buttons and tried it on.

'You look fabulous,' she said. 'And it fits perfectly. Go and take a look.'

He walked into the hall and stood in front of the full-length mirror. 'Yeah, it looks good. What will you be wearing?'

'I didn't want us to clash, so I'll be wearing a dress in that colour,' she said, pointing to one of the shades of blue on his shirt. It was a dress she had been lucky enough to find in a sale and couldn't resist. A dress she had bought specifically for Daniel's party.

'So you're thinking of us as a couple?' he teased.

Was that what she'd been thinking when she bought the dress? Her first thought had been how well the colour would look next to Daniel's shirt.

There was only one way to deal with his suggestion. 'Of course I am!' she laughed, once again using laughter as a shield to protect her feelings.

She turned away and walked back into the kitchen, busying herself with the box and the wrapping. Too scared that her eyes would reveal the pain in her heart.

SIXTEEN

They took a walk down by the river the following afternoon, taking what had become their usual route. Abby was relieved to see Adam's bench was free.

She told Daniel how she had sat there when he was away, thinking about Adam's unfulfilled dream of walking her down the aisle. 'I still feel a bit guilty about it.'

'I don't think you should. You had the reception for everyone. Adam gave his speech. He danced with you as father-of-the-bride. They're the memories to hold onto, Abby. Not the things that didn't happen.'

'I know. I just think we could have done it better.'

'But you had the wedding that was right for you.'

She stared at him in surprise. 'You've never said that to me before. What do you mean? You think we were playing games? You don't think we were in love?'

'No, I've never thought that. I just meant it was an unplanned, spur-of-the-moment kind of wedding. I'm not sure either of you were committed enough to go for a formal church do.'

She was shocked and hurt by this revelation. Without giving herself time to think she blurted out her next words.

'And you would know all about that, Daniel. You're the expert on commitment, aren't you?'

She regretted her words as soon as they had left her mouth and wished she could take them back. This was not how she had intended it to come out. How on earth could they talk about it calmly and reasonably after that? She had ruined everything.

Her eyes were fixed on the ground at her feet. 'I can't do this,' she said. She stood up and walked away from him, trying desperately to compose herself before he confirmed what she had just alluded to.

But Daniel had no clue of the true meaning behind her words. He had heard the sarcasm in her voice and assumed it was just a 'pot calling kettle' moment, since his own track record on commitment had been no better than Abby's.

'What's happened, Abby?' he asked when he caught up with her. 'I never meant to upset you.'

She was relieved that he seemed to have no idea what she'd been trying to say, and attempted to give him an explanation. 'It wasn't you exactly. It's just that your words were a trigger.'

He turned to look at her, moving his face close to hers. For a moment she thought he was going to kiss her. It was too much. 'Don't,' she said, turning away.

'Don't what? I just want to help you.' He was convinced it had something to do with Gavin, but after her initial reaction he wouldn't bring up her marriage for a second time. 'Please tell me what's wrong.'

Tell him that the thought of losing him to someone else was tearing her apart? How could she possibly tell him that?

'Abby, please. I hate seeing you so unhappy.'

She knew this wasn't the right time to burden him with her thoughts. Not when she was so upset. Her words would come out wrong. And she had already said too much. If she kept going, she would come across as selfish and uncaring. The opposite of how she wanted to be. But she had to tell him something.

'I'll be okay,' she said. 'You know me, I can get a bit emotional at times.' She gave him a smile, but he could see the sadness in her eyes and wasn't convinced by her reply.

He took hold of her hand, and they continued their walk in silence until they reached the footbridge over the weir. Abby leant against the railings and looked down at the scene below where the ducks balanced fearlessly as the cascading water swept over their webbed feet. She found the noise strangely comforting.

Daniel moved his head closer to hers as she began to speak, the loud rushing sound of the water almost drowning out her words.

'There *has* been something on my mind,' she said. 'Something that I'm finding difficult to handle. But I'd rather not talk about it right now, if that's okay.'

'I'm here whenever you're ready.'

'What I'd really love is a hug.'

With his hands resting lightly on her shoulders, he turned her round to face him. He asked no questions, not wanting to betray her trust in him. Just quietly accepted that sometimes there would be things she found difficult to talk to him about. It worked both ways, of course. He knew first-hand that some things were much harder to reveal than others.

As she felt Daniel's arms enveloping her, Abby closed her eyes and breathed him in. Each passing second became locked inside her memory for the times when he would no longer be beside her. She felt her negativity slowly draining away.

SEVENTEEN

Friday was the start of their long weekend to celebrate Daniel's birthday. They began their journey just after nine o'clock. The early morning mist had cleared, revealing a cloudless blue sky and bright sunshine. 'Let's hope it's like this by the coast,' Abby said.

'They're predicting rain for Saturday night,' Daniel said. 'But we should be okay for the barbecue.'

'I hope we get a chance to have a walk on the beach. It's been so long since I've seen the sea.'

'Then we'll make sure we fit in a walk today. And right now I think it's time we continued our alphabet game.'

'Yes, I think we should.'

It was no surprise to Abby that Daniel had his words ready: 'Kaleidoscope Kisses.'

Her mind conjured up colourful images of fireworks exploding into the dark night as romantic couples kissed under the stars. 'Well, I'm sure the birthday boy will be getting plenty of those,' she smiled.

'I shall look forward to that,' he grinned.

'Just to clarify, I'm not talking about me.'

'But it's my birthday!'

'Maybe just a little one. Although you'll have to wait until Sunday for that. I was talking about the women who'll be at your party.' *Georgia, for instance.*

'You think they'll all be lining up for a kiss, do you?'

'They might be.'

'As long as that's all they're after,' he laughed.

For Abby this was further confirmation that there was someone he had left behind in Canada. Someone who would have the power to change the relationship between herself and Daniel if she chose to. But Abby was not going to spoil Daniel's birthday weekend by fretting over things she could do nothing about.

'So you think you'll be able to resist all those Longing Looks?' she asked.

'Very good,' he smiled.

'You never know, maybe something will turn up when you least expect it. When you're not even looking,' she said, paraphrasing Daniel's words to her when she had jokingly referred to his Ms Right.

He turned to look at her, wondering if she had been hinting at something. But with her eyes shielded behind her sunglasses and focused on the road ahead, there was nothing he could read from her expression.

'What about you?' he asked. 'What are you hoping for?'

'Me? I'm just a girl who wants to have fun.'

'Then how about some music we can sing along to?'

'Okay. You choose.'

'Play *Mr Brightside*,' Daniel requested.

'Yes!' Abby shouted as the familiar guitar intro began to

play.

They spent the rest of the journey singing along to songs from the past and the present, taking turns to pick their favourites or ones with a special memory for them both, laughing and joking when they forgot the words. The fun had already started.

They arrived at their destination around half past twelve. 'This house is amazing,' Abby said as Daniel pulled up outside his parents' home.

Olivia came out to greet them and there were hugs all round. 'Lucy is already here with the family,' she said. 'They're down on the beach at the moment. We'll be having an alfresco lunch at one o'clock.'

'And here we have Abby's contribution,' Daniel said, taking a cool bag from the back of the car and passing it to Abby.

'Wonderful. Thank you so much,' Olivia said, slipping her arm into Abby's and walking with her into the house. 'It's good to see you on a happier occasion, Abby.'

'It's lovely to be here. The house is beautiful, and such a stunning location.'

'Yes. We've grown very fond of it.' They stopped near the stairs and Olivia took the cool bag from Abby. 'I'll take this into the kitchen. Would you like to freshen up before lunch?'

'Yes. Thank you. I won't be long.'

'I've put Abby across the corridor from your room,' Olivia said to Daniel as he walked in with their luggage.

'Right.' He passed Abby her holdall. 'I'll show you the way,' he said, carrying her small suitcase and his bag up the impressive wooden staircase, then turning left at the top. 'There are four bedrooms down here. We have the two at the end. Mine has a sea view and the sun. I'd be happy to swap if you want to.'

'Thanks. But I'm not taking your room, Daniel.'

He opened the door into her room and she stepped inside. 'Oh, this is gorgeous,' she said, genuinely delighted by what she saw. The sage green walls, lilac rugs and coordinating soft furnishings softened the boldness of the oak furniture and parquet flooring, giving the room a warm and cosy vibe.

'I've not seen it since it's been redecorated. It looks good,' Daniel said from the doorway.

Abby put her bag down on the bed and looked around. 'Are those cupboards?' she asked, pointing to two doors on the opposite wall.

'The one on the right is a wardrobe. The one on the left is the en suite.'

'Really? I have my own bathroom?'

'Says the woman with three toilets, two showers and one spa bath in her solo flat,' he grinned.

'Okay! I just didn't know what to expect. You've never really talked much about it other than the location.'

'When they bought it there was a storage room at the end of the corridor which they didn't want, so they had it transformed into two bathrooms.'

'That makes sense,' she said, opening the door through

to the en suite. 'This is lovely.'

Daniel wheeled in her suitcase. 'I'll be in my room when you're ready,' he said, closing the door behind him.

Within a few minutes, Abby was walking through the open door into Daniel's room. 'Very nice,' she said. The teal blue on the walls and the dark grey furniture were a complete change from the room she had just left, but the effect was just as pleasing.

'Did you have a say in the decorating?' she asked.

'No. The last time I was here for more than a couple of nights was the summer before I emigrated, so over eleven years ago.'

After university, Daniel had spent eighteen months working and travelling across Canada, falling in love with the vast open spaces and spectacular scenery, the vibrant cities and culture. All of which would later become the inspiration for his first published novel. It was inevitable that within a year he would return there to live.

Abby had been the one to see him off at the airport on that first trip. The first of many goodbyes and hellos they had been through over the years. And in a little over two weeks they would be saying goodbye once again. It had become a familiar part of their lives.

She walked across to the window and opened it wide, taking in the sea air and the salt breeze. The beach was hidden from view, but the enchanting sound of children's laughter mixed with waves breaking on the shore reached up to her from below. 'It's so beautiful here,' she said. 'They chose a wonderful place to retire.'

'You never know, maybe I'll end up doing the same thing.'

'I think that's a lovely idea,' she said, turning round to face him. But she had no idea what part there would be for herself in his future plans. Perhaps he would see her as nothing more than an occasional visitor. Two old friends comfortably re-hashing old memories in their twilight years.

There would be no extended holiday together. No chance of a romantic happy ending on a faraway island. Didn't she have to accept that their dreams were not the same?

He was holding her gaze, the same look on his face as he'd had before. The look that told her he had a secret to reveal. 'Come and sit down,' he said, gesturing for her to sit beside him on the sofa.

She turned back to the window for one more look at the sea, not yet ready to hear what he had to say. Relieved that she had a valid excuse. 'I think it's time I went to help Olivia.'

Reluctantly he stood up. 'No, you're right. She'll be wondering what's happened to us.'

EIGHTEEN

Abby had been expecting a cosy farmhouse-style kitchen and was surprised to find a modern open-plan space, split into kitchen, dining and lounge areas, with folding glass doors leading onto the patio. Olivia was sitting at a kitchen table large enough to seat eight, chatting with a woman her own age who Abby didn't know. But Daniel clearly did.

'Hello, Daniel,' the woman said as they walked in. 'It's so lovely to see you.'

'You too, Deborah,' he smiled.

Olivia introduced Abby as 'Daniel's childhood friend' and Deborah as 'my close friend who lives next door'.

'Is there anything I can do?' Abby asked.

'We're just waiting for the others to come up from the beach, then we'll start taking the food out,' Olivia said.

'And is Roger here?' Daniel asked.

'Yes, he's on the beach with Greg and the others,' Deborah said. 'And there's someone else who wanted to say hello. I hope you don't mind.'

As if summoned by Deborah's words, a woman in her early thirties came through from the garden. Petite with dark hair expertly cut to just above her shoulders, dressed in skinny jeans and a close-fitting T-shirt.

Daniel had his back to the door and didn't notice she was there until he heard her speak. 'Well, look who it is. Daniel Stratton, serial heartbreaker. So you finally decided to come back for me?'

He turned round, recognising her instantly. 'Eva,' he grinned. 'How are you?'

'As if you care,' she smiled, putting her arms around his neck and pulling his head down until his lips met hers for a quick kiss.

Then her eyes found Abby. 'And you must be Abby. The one woman Daniel refuses to give up.'

'Hello, Eva. It's lovely to meet you.'

'You too,' Eva said, giving Abby a hug. 'So have you managed to tame him?'

'Is that possible?' Abby laughed. 'I stay out of it.'

Eva turned back to Daniel. 'Am I finally going to get an apology for being carelessly thrown aside after our ten days of non-stop amazing sex?'

'Eva, really. We don't need to hear that,' Deborah said, her cheeks reddening.

'For goodness sake, Mum. What did you think we were doing all those hours I spent over here?'

It was no surprise to Abby. She remembered Daniel telling her years ago about the sexy neighbour who had been the reason for him staying longer at his parents' house than he had intended.

'It was nothing more than a fun holiday romance,' Daniel said. 'I no more broke your heart than you broke mine.'

'But I didn't know then that you were going to be famous. I would have enjoyed the celebrity lifestyle and spending some of that lovely money.'

Deborah shook her head, exasperated with her daughter, but Eva was used to her mother's disapproval. It had no effect on her at all.

'I think you have an inflated view of my wealth and status,' Daniel laughed. 'You would have been bored to tears. How about an invite to my party tomorrow. Will that do?'

'That will be perfect,' Eva smiled. Her mission successful.

A long trestle table had been set up on the patio for their alfresco lunch. Abby was seated between Daniel and Lucy, with Eva on the other side of Daniel. Eva was doing most of the talking, filling Daniel in on what she had been up to over the missing years. For the past five, she had been working in London for a top advertising agency.

'Do you fancy a walk to the pub later?' Abby heard Daniel say. When he paused and then said her name, she realised he was actually talking to her.

She turned to face him. 'Yes, okay.'

'Great.'

Olivia was sitting opposite and had heard every word. 'That's a good idea,' she said. 'I'll look after the children.'

'What's this?' Angus asked.

'Daniel has suggested a visit to the pub this evening,'

Olivia said.

'What do you think?' Angus asked Lucy. 'Shall we go?

'Yes, count us in.'

'Sounds good,' Eva said, not wanting to miss out.

It wasn't exactly what Daniel had in mind when he made the suggestion, but he was happy to go along with the new plan. With so many people around this weekend, he realised it would be prudent to wait until Sunday afternoon before speaking to Abby. When he could be certain that there would be no interruptions.

Abby had her longed-for walk along the beach after lunch. She chatted with Lucy as the two children ran on ahead, closely followed by Daniel and Angus. Joseph and Ruby were full of energy, laughing as they dodged the chasing waves, then squealing with delight as they were caught by their father or Daniel and lifted high into the air.

'Daniel is wonderful with Joseph and Ruby,' Lucy said as they watched the scene in front of them. 'Has he still not shown any signs of wanting to settle down himself?'

'He seems more concerned about my own single status at the moment,' Abby said, successfully navigating the question. 'He's forever teasing me about it.'

'And are *you* concerned?'

'No. After one failed marriage, I'm not ready for another committed relationship. I like to have fun, but any sign that they're after something more meaningful is a red flag for me.'

'I remember those dating days,'' Lucy said. 'Our life is

very different now, but neither of us would have it any other way.' They came to a stop as the others began to make their way back. 'Have you ever thought of you and Daniel being friends with benefits?'

'Where did that come from?' Abby asked, laughing awkwardly.

'Sorry, was that too much?'

'No, it's fine. If I'm honest, the thought has crossed my mind. But it's a complete non-starter. It would ruin our friendship.'

'You're probably right. Especially since you've been friends for so long. Do you know if he's bringing someone to the party?'

'He's not mentioned anything to me.'

'Who are we talking about?' Angus asked as they came within earshot.

'I was just wondering if Daniel has a date for tomorrow night,' Lucy said.

'I'm going with Abby,' Daniel said, winking at Abby. 'She's bought us matching outfits.'

'No I haven't! All I said was I didn't want us to clash. If you want to take someone else, I have no problem with that.'

'How about Eva?' Angus said. 'She's pretty…' He hesitated, deciding it would probably be better if he didn't finish the sentence.

But Lucy wouldn't let him get away with it. She raised her eyebrows. 'Pretty what, Angus? Hot?'

'I was going to say she's pretty well-suited to Daniel.'

He took hold of Lucy's hand and pulled her towards him. 'And you are pretty perfect for me,' he said, wrapping his arms around her and giving her a kiss.

'Nice save, mate,' Daniel laughed. 'Actually, Eva and I have a bit of a history. We spent a couple of weeks together over a decade ago. But I'm not interested in going down that road again.'

'And does Eva feel the same?' Lucy asked.

'She does. She was asking me at lunch if there would be any single guys at the party I could introduce her to.'

Lucy suddenly felt a tug on her T-shirt. 'I'm hungry,' Joseph said.

Ruby joined in. 'Me too.'

Lucy crouched down to their level. 'How about we go back to the house? If you ask her very nicely, Aunty Liv might find something for you to eat.'

'Yay,' they cried in unison, jumping up and down.

'We'll see you later,' Lucy said, taking hold of Joseph's hand as Angus swung Ruby onto his shoulders.

'Did you grill Lucy about married life?' Daniel asked as they watched the family running towards the steps, the children squealing with delight.

'Of course not. Anyway, I didn't need to. It's obvious how happy they are.'

He put his arm loosely around her shoulders and they turned towards the horizon. 'Have you enjoyed your walk along the beach?' he asked.

'I have. It's been wonderful.'

'How about getting a bit closer to the sea?'

Before she realised what he was thinking, he picked her up and threw her over his shoulder.

'Daniel, don't you dare,' she shrieked. 'Put me down!'

He stopped at the water's edge, then lowered her feet onto the wet sand. 'You didn't really think I'd do it, did you?'

'I'm never quite sure *what* you're going to do.'

'That's what keeps me interesting,' he grinned.

She smiled up at him. 'Just one of the things I love about you.'

He smiled back but said nothing further, slipped his hands into his pockets and turned to face the house. Abby leant against him, and he absentmindedly kissed her on top of her head. She took hold of his arm, and they made their way back to the steps in reflective silence.

NINETEEN

On Saturday morning, Abby joined Olivia and Greg in the kitchen just after eight o'clock. They greeted each other warmly, and Greg poured Abby a coffee. She declined the offer of breakfast, preferring to wait for Daniel. 'Am I the first one down?' she asked.

'Yes, you are,' Olivia said. 'The children always sleep longer when they're by the sea.'

'How was your trip to the pub last night?' Greg asked.

'It was good, thanks. We played darts for most of the time, which was a lot of fun.'

'And how did you find Eva?'

'I really liked her. She's great company.'

'Yes, there's never a dull moment with Eva around,' Greg said with a chuckle.

Olivia pursed her lips, resisting the urge to comment.

They chatted about the plans for the day. Olivia had organised everything down to the last detail, but could do nothing about the weather. 'They're forecasting a storm in the early hours,' she said. 'The taxis are scheduled for two. But if the storm hits before then, they might have to arrive earlier.'

'What we don't want is to wake up with a houseful of hung-over guests,' Greg said.

But Abby reassured him. 'Don't worry. I'll make sure it doesn't come to that.'

'Thank you,' Olivia smiled. 'You were always the sensible one.'

Abby thought it made her sound boring. Is that how people saw her? She could be fun, but she was never going to be a Georgia or an Eva. Never going to be the life and soul of the party, grabbing everyone's attention. But she was happy with who she was. Proud of the independent woman she had become. And nothing was going to stop her having fun tonight.

As well as Asha and Rakesh, five of Daniel's closest friends were there for the lunchtime barbecue: three with their partners, and two singles. Lucy and Angus would not be joining them. They had taken the children out for the afternoon.

Abby was sitting on the patio, chatting with some of the guests. Other people had congregated near the barbecue, where Greg was taking charge of the cooking. 'Five minutes,' they all heard him shout.

'That's my cue,' Olivia said, getting up and going inside.

'I'll come and help,' Abby said. Asha also stood up, and followed her friend into the kitchen.

As they were bringing salads and bread to the table, Abby and Asha overheard some of the conversation from Daniel's friends. Specifically Matt, who had a lot to say about how his life had changed for the better after meeting Thérése. 'What about you, Daniel,' he asked. 'Thinking of settling down yet?'

But someone else butted in before Daniel had a chance to answer. 'Daniel? You must be joking. The thought of committing himself to one woman for the rest of his life would terrify him.' There was a general burst of laughter.

'I'm still here,' Daniel said, a bit put out. 'God knows how I managed to get this reputation. I was no worse than the rest of you at uni.'

'Not me,' Matt said.

'Nor me,' Rakesh said. 'I always knew Asha was the one.'

'Troy, will you back me up here?' Daniel asked.

'It's all a total blur,' Troy laughed.

Daniel gave a sigh. 'Maybe I'll surprise you all. I could be ready to settle down sooner than you think.'

'Now do you believe me?' Abby whispered to Asha on their way back to the kitchen.

Asha had to admit there could be more to Abby's theory than she had first thought.

When everyone was seated round the table, Abby found herself next to Matt, whom she had met several times before. 'You know I always fancied you,' he told her.

'You did?' she laughed. 'I had no idea.'

'But you were off limits, obviously, being Daniel's girl.'

'I was never Daniel's girl. Is that what he told you?'

'Not exactly. He told us you were his best friend. But he made it obvious that he wouldn't like it if any of us asked you out. And you're still in his life. For Daniel, that's very telling. He obviously cares about you a lot.'

'We've known each other since primary school, so we've always had a connection. We do love each other, but just as friends. It's a world away from being *in* love.' She gave him a smile. 'Of course, you would know all about that.'

'Yeah, she's amazing,' he said, looking across at Thérése. 'Everything I could have wished for.' Then he lowered his voice. 'Now we're just waiting for Daniel to admit he's found someone.'

At that moment Daniel looked up, caught Abby's eye and smiled. She gave him a smile back, but in her mind she was wondering how much time was left before secrets were revealed. Before her relationship with Daniel would be changed forever.

Two six-seater taxis arrived at four o'clock to take everyone back to the hotel, and a temporary peace descended on the house. Although it seemed to Abby to be a rather premature ending to the barbecue, she understood why Greg and Olivia had wanted a break. It was a chance to unwind, to recharge, before the main event.

Lucy and Angus returned a short while later, and Olivia suggested they relax in the snug with the children while the rest of them were clearing away.

'Is the snug as cosy as it sounds?' Abby asked as she was emptying the plates ready for Olivia to stack into the dishwasher.

'Yes, it's one of my favourite spaces,' Olivia said. 'Comfy sofas and a relaxing ambience. It's where we spend the evenings when it's just the two of us, either reading or watching television. I'm surprised Daniel hasn't shown you round the downstairs rooms.'

'I actually have no idea where the party is going to be.'

'Then I'll ask him to show you once they've finished outside. He's never been very fond of the room, but I think he'll like the small changes that have been made for tonight.'

'Do you use it often?'

'No. We have a Christmas party there every year, but for smaller dinner parties with family or friends we prefer to use this room.'

Daniel and Greg came in from the garden. 'All done,' Greg said. 'We've battened down the hatches. Any updates on the weather?'

'No. They're still saying yellow warning for three in the morning,' Olivia said. She turned to Daniel, 'Would you like to show Abby the party room before tonight?'

'We can take a look now,' he said.

Abby followed Daniel into the hall. 'Is the room very grand?' she asked.

'I find it oppressive with the dark green over the walls and ceiling. It's not to my taste at all. But it's the perfect size for a party.'

As they entered the dining room they saw hundreds of tiny lights on the ceiling, looking spectacular against the dark green surface. The mahogany dining table had been placed in the window alcove, covered with gold-coloured tablecloths in readiness for the buffet, with curtains of lights hung behind.

The partition in the centre had been folded back, revealing a sitting room, and almost doubling the space. The French windows that led onto the patio were also hung with a curtain of lights.

'Daniel, this is wonderful,' Abby said.

'Yeah, it looks good. The lights have transformed it.'

She walked through to the far end. 'And it would be perfect for a summer party with the doors opening out onto the garden.'

'You want to book it for your thirty-fifth, do you?' he chuckled.

'Actually, I quite like that idea. I'll give it some thought.' She turned to face him. 'As long as you promise to be there.'

'Where else would I be on such an auspicious day?' he asked. His voice was light, teasing her.

But, to Abby, his question was an important one. And she had no idea what the answer was going to be.

TWENTY

Abby stood in front of the full-length mirror, checking her appearance from all angles. The short dress fitted her well. Dark blue, spaghetti straps, and with faux feathers in a lighter blue around the top. Her hair was up with two curls hanging at the front, framing her face. She smiled at her reflection, happy with what she saw.

But it had gone half past eight. Daniel would be waiting for her in the corridor.

He was standing there as she opened the bedroom door. 'You look gorgeous,' he said.

'Thank you. So do you.'

'The perfect matching couple,' he grinned.

'And we are going to have a lot of fun celebrating your birthday,' she said. 'Are you ready?'

'I'm ready.' He took hold of her hand, and they made their way downstairs.

It wasn't long before the party guests started arriving. Abby's friends all arrived together, Georgia wearing a daring calf-length turquoise dress with straps across the bodice, covering her nipples but not much else, and a split up the side. She had the confidence to carry it off perfectly. Abby thought she looked stunning.

Ellie and Georgia were delighted to finally meet Daniel. Georgia insisted on a selfie, then asked Abby to take a full-length picture as she posed provocatively against him, her exposed leg wrapped between his. 'Don't we look a gorgeous couple,' she laughed.

Daniel smiled obligingly for the two photos, then excused himself. There were other people he wanted to greet.

Once everyone had a drink in their hands, Greg tapped his glass and made a toast. Olivia had implored him to keep it short, but Daniel could have done without it altogether.

Greg thanked everyone for coming, and thanked Olivia for arranging the party. He said how proud they both were of Daniel's success, and how pleasant it had been to spend a few days with him after such a long time apart. Then he raised his glass and encouraged everyone to do the same, all wishing Daniel a happy birthday.

'You see, there was nothing to worry about,' Abby whispered. 'It was a lovely toast.'

'It wasn't bad. At least he didn't insist on a round of *Happy Birthday*.'

'Now there's a thought,' Abby smiled.

'Don't you dare!'

Greg and Olivia stayed at the party until ten o'clock, Olivia taking charge of the buffet. They stopped to speak with Daniel and Lucy before withdrawing upstairs to their room.

'Mum's just told us they'll be doing brunch at eleven,' Daniel told Abby. 'Do you think you can make that?'

'I'm sure I can,' she said. 'Now, don't you think it's time for you to mingle? You have a lot of catching up to do.'

But before Abby could turn away he took hold of her hand. 'Save a dance for me.'

She gave him a warm smile. 'Of course.'

A group of people, mostly singles, had gathered in the lounge area to play drinking games. Abby noticed Daniel going to join them, but she wasn't tempted. She was going to have fun on the dance floor.

There was a lot of singing, a lot of interaction with everyone. Inhibitions were left behind. The party was just getting started.

Towards the end of the evening, Abby found herself in the arms of Matt. Daniel was dancing with Thérése. And Abby noticed Eva enjoying herself immensely with Daniel's cousin, Dean.

'It's been a brilliant weekend,' Matt said. 'We're hoping to see Daniel again before he returns to Canada. We've invited him to come and stay with us in London. And the invitation extends to you, too.'

'Thanks. I'd love to come.'

'Great. We'll arrange something next week.'

Thérése gave Daniel a quick kiss on the cheek when the song had ended. 'It's been a wonderful party,' she said. 'Thank you so much.' She smiled up at Matt. 'And now

I'm going to reclaim my gorgeous fiancé.'

Daniel turned to Abby. 'Shall we?' he said, and she stepped into his open arms.

'Have you had fun tonight?' she asked.

'I have,' he said. 'It's been fantastic.'

'And I've had a wonderful time.'

'I could tell,' he smiled. 'I was starting to worry that I wasn't going to get my dance.'

'As if I'd turn down the birthday boy,' she smiled. 'But you do have a fabulous group of friends.'

'Did you know Matt was completely smitten with you back in the day?'

'So he told me. He also said you wouldn't have liked it if he'd asked me out.'

'He's right. It would have made things very awkward.'

'Just remember that the next time Georgia is flaunting herself in front of you.'

'I have no interest in pursuing anything with Georgia.'

No, of course he hadn't. She knew that. And she knew why. She blocked out those thoughts as he held her close, and they gently swayed to the music. She could only guess what changes the future would bring to their lives, but right now she would just enjoy this precious moment with her best friend.

TWENTY-ONE

It was two o'clock, and the party was coming to an end. There were still two taxis waiting outside to take people back to the hotel. Abby knew Asha and Rakesh had already left. She saw Ellie and Jon looking ready to leave and went over to them. 'Have you enjoyed yourselves?' she asked.

'It's been great, Abby,' Ellie said. 'You'll thank Daniel for us, won't you?'

'Yes, I will,' she said, giving them both a hug. 'Thanks so much for coming.' But she had no idea where Daniel was at that moment. And there was someone else missing, too. 'Have you seen Georgia?' she asked.

'I think she needed the bathroom,' Jon said.

'Okay, thanks.'

When they had left, Abby went into the snug and picked up Georgia's coat. It suddenly occurred to her that Georgia may have had too much to drink and was feeling unwell. She quickly made her way to the bathroom, but stopped in her tracks when she reached the door.

There was some very loud moaning coming from inside. But not the moans of somebody feeling nauseous.

This person sounded euphoric. Abby was convinced it was Georgia. Georgia did nothing quietly, why should sex be any different?

'Please don't let it be Daniel,' she whispered. Unwilling to investigate further, she retraced her steps down the corridor. But as she turned the corner she bumped straight into him. 'You're here!' she gasped with relief. 'I've been looking for you.'

'I've been outside organising the transport. The wind's picking up, which means the storm is on its way, and there's still one taxi waiting to leave. We're missing Troy and Georgia. Any ideas?'

'Georgia's in the bathroom. I assume it must be Troy in there with her.'

'You mean they're having sex?'

'It sounds like it.'

'They're staying in the same hotel, for God's sake. Couldn't they have waited?' He ran down the corridor and knocked loudly on the bathroom door. 'You need to come out now.'

'Give us a minute,' Georgia giggled.

'Now!' Daniel said. Getting no further response, he opened the unlocked door and found Georgia and Troy hurriedly attempting to make themselves decent.

'Excuse me!' Georgia said, giggling again.

'You need to leave,' Daniel said. 'The last taxi's waiting and won't be waiting for much longer. You need to get back to the hotel. The weather's getting worse.'

'Sorry, mate,' Troy said. 'We got a bit carried away. You

know how it is.'

'I'm ready,' Georgia said, walking towards the door. 'Did you enjoy looking at my boobs, Daniel Stratton?'

'I didn't even notice,' he lied.

'Well aren't you the perfect gentleman?' She reached up and gave him a kiss. 'It was a lovely party. Thank you for inviting me.'

'You're welcome. Now, can we go?'

Abby helped Georgia on with her coat and steered her swiftly to the front door, closely followed by Daniel and Troy.

'My new man is gorgeous, don't you think?' Georgia said in a loud whisper.

'We'll talk about it later,' Abby said, giving Georgia a hug. 'I'll see you soon.'

'You think you'll have time to come to London?' Troy asked.

'I'll be in touch,' Daniel said, just wanting them to leave. He stood under the porch with Abby until Georgia and Troy were safely on board, much to the relief of the other passengers, and the taxi had driven away. As it vanished round the corner the rain began to fall.

'Are you ready to go up?' he asked as they stepped back inside. 'I just need to check the doors. I won't be long.'

'I'll wait for you in the kitchen.'

Abby stood by the glass doors as the rain fell harder and the garden began to lose its grip against the wind. But her thoughts were not on the weather. She had decided this would be the perfect time for the truth to come out. They had both been procrastinating for far too long.

She would tell him what she suspected and give him the chance to confirm or deny it, however painful his words might be.

A few minutes later, she heard his footsteps entering the room. 'All safe and secure,' he said.

She turned to face him, unwavering in her resolve to go through with her decision.

'Are you ready to go up?' he asked once again.

'Not yet. I think it's time for us to talk, Daniel.'

He didn't question her words. Not when it was also something he wanted. 'Shall I go first?'

'No, I'd like to. If that's okay.' She had already worked out how she was going to start. She held on to his hands and took a deep breath. 'I know, Daniel.'

'What do you know?' he asked softly.

'I know that you've fallen in love.'

He was taken aback by her statement, had he made it that obvious? But there was also enormous relief that it was finally going to be out in the open. 'How did you guess?'

It was not the response she had been hoping for. She had clung to the faint possibility that he would deny it. That she had got it all wrong and things would be as they had always been. But she saw the sparkle in his eyes. Saw the joy he couldn't hide from his face. There was no going back now.

'I've been wondering about it for a while, but I couldn't

be certain,' she said. 'It was seeing you today, seeing the way you were with women who were obviously attracted to you. It was clear to me that you weren't interested in getting cosy with any of them. And that's when I knew I was right.'

'And how do you feel about that?'

'I'm finding it difficult to accept.'

'Would it help if we talked about it?'

She shook her head, knowing that it wouldn't help at all. She was embarrassed and ashamed at how she was feeling. She should be congratulating him, asking him all those questions that normal friends would ask. Finding out all she could about the new woman in his life. But not yet. It was too new. Too soon.

'I'd rather not,' she said. 'I need time to let it sink in.'

'That's fine. I understand, Abby. I can wait.'

She *was* happy for him, but she needed to be honest as well. 'I don't want it to spoil our friendship. I couldn't bear that.'

She felt his thumbs gently caressing the back of her hands as he tried to reassure her. 'We won't let it spoil anything, Abby.'

'So have you explained about us?'

'What are you talking about?'

'Does she know about me? About how close we are?'

She was making no sense at all. 'Does who know?'

'Your girlfriend, of course,' she said, laughing nervously.

'My girlfriend?'

'The one you've just told me you're in love with.'

He stared at her, and she watched his face go from a puzzled frown to sudden realisation. 'Abby, I was talking about you. I'm hopelessly in love with you.'

It was Abby's turn to stare, her blank expression hiding the conflicting thoughts colliding in her brain. The elation she felt on hearing his words, battling against the desperate pain of knowing a romantic relationship between them could never last.

'I love you too, Daniel,' she whispered, unable to think of anything else to say. His words had been so unexpected. How could this be happening?

Of course, it wasn't the first time she had told him she loved him. But there was something in the way she said it that made him dare to believe she was feeling the same emotions as he was right now.

'Can I kiss you?' he asked. It was a question he had been avoiding for almost two decades.

She knew exactly what he meant. He wasn't talking about a peck on the cheek or a quick meeting of the lips. He was talking about a full-blown kiss. It was her chance to discover how it would feel. Just one kiss. Surely one kiss wouldn't do any harm?

She took a step forward, their bodies touching. It felt so good. So right. Her eyes locked onto his. 'Happy birthday,' she whispered.

He didn't need any more encouragement. He wrapped his arms around her waist, pulling her closer as his lips moved down to hers, at first his tongue gently exploring, then the passion growing more intense.

She was swept away by the sheer joy of it, by the way he tasted, the way his body felt against her. It was a moment that she would keep locked in her heart forever. The most intimate moment they had ever shared.

'That was beautiful,' he whispered as their lips finally parted.

She rested her head against his chest, listening to the beat of his heart. Her body ached for him, but her feelings scared her. 'I think I should go,' she said.

He wasn't surprised by her words. Hadn't he always known she was afraid of risking their friendship? There was a chance she wouldn't want to talk about it tomorrow, just go back to the easy way they had with each other as if nothing had happened. If only he could make her see that they wouldn't be risking anything. They would be adding so much more to what they already had.

In spite of her words, she hadn't left. He stood perfectly still, wanting to preserve the moment for as long as he could. But there was no more time.

'I must go. I'm sorry,' she whispered, grasping his hand as she stepped away from him.

'Don't be sorry, Abby. I understand.'

She walked backwards towards the door, slowly releasing his hand until only their fingertips were touching. When the connection was lost, she turned and left the room without looking back.

Daniel remained in the kitchen, watching the storm raging outside whilst trying to calm the thoughts inside his head. He could still taste her on his tongue, still feel her body pressing against him. There had been so much passion in their kiss. He knew she had felt it, too. Had it always been there for her as well as for him?

As a teenager he had refused to acknowledge the extent of his love for Abby. Somehow it had felt wrong, and he had pushed those feelings away. In the years that followed he had gradually realised there was no other woman he could love the way he loved her, until he had finally decided to stop looking.

He had two and a half weeks. Two and a half weeks to convince her to change her mindset. But it was a challenge far harder than working out a new plot for a novel. This time he had no idea how it was going to end.

TWENTY-TWO

Abby slept for a few hours, despite the sound of the wind howling through the trees and the rain lashing against the window. When she awoke, just before nine o'clock, the wind had died down but the rain was falling fast. There would be no repeat of their walk along the beach.

She took her time getting showered and dressed, and left her room at twenty to eleven. Pausing outside Daniel's door, there was only silence. Should she knock and check if he was awake? She decided against it. He still had twenty minutes. Or he may already be downstairs.

There was a warm smell like roast potatoes wafting from the kitchen, and she could hear voices. But not Daniel's. She found Greg and Olivia seated at the kitchen table with Joseph and Ruby, who were eating their breakfast.

'Morning,' Abby smiled.

'Good morning,' Greg said. 'Coffee?'

'I'd love some. Thank you.'

'Did you manage to sleep through the storm?'

'Yes, I slept very well. The bed was so comfortable.'

'And how was the party?' Olivia asked.

'It was fabulous. Thank you for all you did, Olivia. Everyone said how much they enjoyed it. And a very dramatic end with the storm blowing in.'

'I trust there were no problems getting back to the hotel?'

'No. I spoke to my friend Ellie last night. Everyone got back safely.'

'That's good to hear. But I expect the weather may change any plans you had for today.'

'Yes, probably. I'll see what Daniel has to say.'

'See what Daniel has to say about what?' he asked, walking into the kitchen. Abby had been trying desperately not to think about their kiss, but on seeing him again she could do nothing to stop the memory taking over her thoughts.

'Happy birthday, darling,' Olivia said, giving him a hug. 'We were just talking about what you'll be doing today in this weather.'

'Yeah, it's not looking good.'

'We have potato wedges with onions, bacon and melted cheese for your birthday brunch. Ready in about fifteen minutes,' Greg said.

'Sounds great,' Daniel said, helping himself to coffee. 'Do you want to go next door?' he asked Abby. 'We could talk about what we're going to do.'

'Yes, okay,' she said, a little nervously, quite sure there would be something else he would want to talk about.

She picked up her mug and followed him into what they called the party room. It had already been cleared, and the furniture put back in its rightful place, but the folding doors remained open.

They walked through to the sitting room and stood in companionable silence by the French windows, looking out onto the wet and windswept garden. Lost in their own, but very similar, thoughts.

Abby was the first to speak. 'I'm happy to go along with whatever you want to do, Daniel. Do you have any ideas?'

'Let's just go back to the flat, then go out in the evening. We could leave in a couple of hours. Hopefully the rain will have eased by then.'

'It's a lot quieter than it was.'

'Did you sleep okay?'

'Yes. How about you?'

He didn't answer her question. Instead he spoke what was on his mind. What had been on his mind since the moment it had happened. 'I hope I wasn't inappropriate with you last night.'

'You mean the kiss?'

'Yes, I mean the kiss.' *And baring my soul.* But he wouldn't mention that just yet. One thing at a time.

Now that it had been brought into the open, Abby found her nerves had vanished. 'Actually, it was lovely,' she said. 'You're a wonderful kisser.' And she gave him one of her beautiful smiles.

He resisted the temptation to take her in his arms and kiss her like that again. But he could feel the tension and anxiety falling away. The relief was immense. 'Momentous

Moments,' he said, smiling back at her.

'Naughty Nights,' she giggled.

He instinctively moved closer to her. 'I could love you so naughty if you'd let me,' he whispered.

But any thoughts of a response she may have given were quashed before she had a chance to speak. 'Brunch is ready,' Greg called from the kitchen.

They left an hour later than planned, choosing to stay behind a little longer with Lucy and Angus. But once they had started the journey, Daniel was impatient to get back. The weather improved as they moved away from the coast and the traffic was light, but it seemed to him to be taking forever.

Now that he had opened up to Abby about his true feelings, he needed to know where he stood. Would she finally be prepared to let go of her conviction that a romantic relationship between them was impossible?

Once Abby had turned off the motorway he took a chance. 'Overt Opinions,' he said. 'Have I convinced you to change yours?'

'No, you haven't. However much I enjoyed kissing you, I won't be changing my mind.'

'What if I extend my stay?'

'There's no need to do that. I'll be coming over to you in December. That's only a few weeks away.' She gave a sad smile. 'Painful Partings.'

But it was no longer a game to Daniel. 'Will you even miss me?' he asked.

'Of course I will. I've got used to you being here.'

'You've got used to me? That's the best reason you can come up with?'

'I didn't mean it like that. You know exactly how I feel about you.'

'I do?'

'You're my best friend, and I love you. I've always told you that.'

'Then why don't we take that love and run with it? Explore the possibilities. We could have something so much more than friendship, Abby.'

'But I'm constantly seeing what can happen when relationships break down. And I've learnt from my own experience how quickly people can grow apart and fall out of love.' She was trying her best to make him understand, but he remained unconvinced.

'What has that got to do with us?'

'We've been through this, Daniel. It's far too risky.'

'So you think it would be better if no-one ever took a chance on love? Honestly, Abby, you have the weirdest sense of logic I've ever come across.'

'I can't help how I feel. I thought you understood.'

'No, I don't understand at all.'

Yes, he knew she loved him. But was it that intense all-consuming love that he felt for her? He was sure he had sensed those same emotions when they had kissed. Had he been completely wrong?

There was nothing left to say from either side, and they sat in silence for the last half hour of their journey.

As Daniel was taking the luggage out of the boot, Abby reached out and took hold of his hand. 'Let's not fight.'

'I don't want to fight either, Abby.'

'Good. It's your birthday. What do you want to do this evening?'

He paused, then gave her a smile. 'Let's wait until we get inside,' he said.

Ten minutes later, they were sitting in the kitchen with a coffee. 'Do you have something planned?' Abby asked. 'You sounded very mysterious in the car park.'

'Tonight is all arranged,' Daniel said, surprising her yet again. 'I've booked a table for us at Castaways.'

'You have? Wow! I love that place. Thank you.'

'Do you go there a lot?'

'No. It's been ages since I was last there. It's quite classy. I'm not sure I have anything to wear.'

'Abby, I've seen your wardrobe,' he laughed.

'You know what I mean. I'm saying I might not have anything *suitable*. It's okay for you. Your biggest decision will be whether to wear a tie or not with your suit.'

'Let me come and help you choose.'

'No, it's okay. I'll manage.'

Her words were hard for him to hear. 'What are you saying? I've opened my heart to you and suddenly you can't trust me? Nothing else will happen unless it's what we both want, Abby.'

Of course she trusted him. But could she trust herself? That was the real issue. She had to ensure their relationship stayed in the friend zone. Anything else could have disastrous consequences.

'Daniel, I'll always trust you. But please don't ask too much of me.'

'All I'm asking is to celebrate my birthday with the woman I love. Drink champagne, enjoy a delicious meal, then take her in my arms and dance the night away.'

'Of course I'll say yes to that. It sounds wonderful.'

'It will be.' Then he grinned at her. 'Tie or no tie?'

'Tie,' she said with a smile.

Abby rediscovered the perfect dress waiting for her in her wardrobe. She had become quite adept at seeking out designer clothes in sales and charity shops. One such item had been waiting patiently for well over a year for a suitable opportunity. A halterneck midi dress in burgundy silk that felt gorgeous against her skin, with a full skirt that swished beautifully when she walked. Castaways with Daniel would be the perfect occasion.

He was waiting for her at the foot of the stairs. 'You look stunning,' he said. 'Definitely worth the wait.'

'I can't believe I forgot I had this dress. I fell in love with it the moment I saw it.'

She gave him a twirl, unaware how her flippant use of the words 'I fell in love' had brought an unexpected jolt of pain to his heart.

TWENTY-THREE

Abby and Daniel stepped into Castaways and into another world. The dimmed lighting, the soft background music, the hushed voices of fellow diners, all combined to create an ambience that was intimate and romantic.

As they sat at their table sipping the chilled champagne that Daniel had pre-ordered, Abby wondered if it had been a mistake to come. How could she possibly resist him in a setting such as this? Was that what he had been thinking when he invited her here?

'When did you book the table?' she asked.

'When I was in Canada. I was always going to spend my birthday with you. I told you that, didn't I?'

'Yes, you did. You also said you hadn't decided what we were going to do.'

'I like surprising you. If the weather had been any different, we could have done something else during the day.'

She knew he was watching her, but she wouldn't look at him. Her eyes were focused on the table. Her fingers fiddling with her napkin.

'Abby, we can leave right now if this is uncomfortable

for you,' he said, reaching across the table and taking her hand in his. 'It may be my birthday, but I don't want to be here if you're not enjoying it.'

She looked up and saw the concern written on his face. 'Thank you,' she said.

'So what do you want to do?'

She gave him a smile. 'I'd like to stay.'

He brought her hand up to his lips, gave it a quick kiss, then laid it back down on the table. It was just a small gesture. A small gesture that she could have no objection to. He would never be overly affectionate with her in public, however romantic the setting. They would enjoy the food and the champagne. Then they would dance together. A perfectly legitimate reason for him to take her in his arms. And a lovely way to end his birthday weekend.

They were just finishing their coffee when the singer stepped onto the small stage. She had a wonderful deep and sensual voice that demanded attention. Daniel stood up, and Abby took hold of his outstretched hand. Then he led her onto the dance floor.

The sublime voice of the singer and the soulful rhythm of the music blended together to create a mood that carried Abby into a dream-like place. With Daniel so close, one hand intertwined with hers, the other round her waist, she laid her head against him and lost herself completely to the moment.

The atmosphere was clearly having an effect on Daniel, too. 'We could be great together, Abby,' he whispered.

'You do know that, don't you?'

Yes, she knew. But how long would it last? There were no guarantees in life. She didn't answer, just moved to the music, not yet ready to wake up from her dream. Because it was only a dream; it could never be their reality. Nothing had changed her mind about that.

As she lifted her head and smiled up at him, he bent his head down and kissed her softly. There was none of the passion of their kiss from the night before, but it was a kiss with more romance than a kiss between friends. A kiss so delicate and lovely. So beautiful.

She had no idea how long they danced or how many songs were sung, but it seemed only minutes from when they had left the table to when loud applause indicated the end of the performance.

Her eyes found his, her face beaming with happiness. 'It's been a wonderful evening, Daniel. Better than I could ever have imagined. Thank you so much.'

'Thank *you*, Abby. There was no-one else I would have wanted to be with tonight.' *Or any other night.* But he kept those words to himself, not wanting to push too far. 'Shall we get a taxi back?' he asked.

'No, let's walk.' She knew she needed to be out in the cool fresh air. Needed time to bring herself back into the real world.

Neither one of them was in a hurry for the evening to end. It was a leisurely walk back to Abby's flat, taking almost twice as long as it had taken to walk to Castaways at the start of the evening.

'Have you enjoyed your birthday weekend?' Abby asked.

'I have. It's been fantastic.'

'And it's so nice that you've reconnected with Olivia and Greg.'

'You know that's down to you, Abby.'

'It was you who made the effort. I just made a suggestion.'

'And what about Troy and Georgia? How long do you give them?'

'I wouldn't be at all surprised if they've already said goodbye, but it would be nice if they lasted a bit longer. I'll no doubt find out all the goss from Georgia.'

'I'll ask Troy for his side of the story when we go down to London. And I need to sort out dates with Matt pretty soon. You're still okay for that, aren't you?'

'Yes, I'm looking forward to it. I don't have any commitments, so I can fit in with you. Do you have any other plans?'

'I'd like to cook a Thanksgiving dinner, and ask Matt and Thérése to join us. And Troy and Georgia, if they're still together. Maybe your other friends, too? And Beth? How many can you fit round the table?'

'Not as many as that! We might have to limit it to six.'

'We can sort something out later this week.'

They took the lift up to the ninth floor. 'Are you tired?' Daniel asked as they let themselves into the flat.

'Actually, I'm wide awake,' Abby said, stepping out of her shoes and hanging up her coat. 'Do you fancy a night cap or a coffee?'

'How about one more dance?'

'Why not?' she giggled. 'I just need to pop upstairs. Choose some music, and I'll be back as quick as I can.'

Daniel found some music they could waltz to. He wanted to take Abby in his arms and twirl her round the floor, something he hadn't been able to do in Castaways or at his party. He took off his jacket and tie, then waited for her to join him.

She took a little longer than she had anticipated, using the time away from him to collect her thoughts and try to put them in a manageable order. He was right. They could be great together. They could be fabulous together, in fact.

As she let her hair down from its clasp, she noticed the change in her reflection. Her eyes had a sparkle to them, and she couldn't stop smiling. She looked happy and in love. Were her reasons for ruling out a romance between them even sustainable anymore? But deep down the fear of losing him if it all went wrong still remained.

Music floated up to her from the hall. She found herself swaying to the beat, imagining herself in Daniel's arms once again.

But when she hadn't reappeared after several minutes, Daniel began to wonder if she had changed her mind. He called up the stairs. 'Abby, are you all right?'

'Just coming,' she called back. What on earth was she doing fantasising in her room when the real thing was waiting for her in the hall?

She walked down the stairs, taking hold of Daniel's

hand for the final two steps, then slipped her shoes back on. They stood facing each other, only a breath away.

He gently pushed her hair behind her ears, took her face in his hands, and kissed her slowly and tenderly. Another kiss that could not be described as an affectionate kiss between friends. And this time she could feel the passion. Feel her heart racing.

They moved together as one, spinning faster and faster as the music reached a crescendo. 'I'm getting dizzy,' she laughed. Coming to a sudden stop, she couldn't prevent herself from stumbling and falling backwards onto the stairs, bringing him down with her.

Their laughter came to an abrupt halt as their eyes met, saying everything they were feeling without the need for words. They both knew instinctively what would happen next. The yearning inside of them was unstoppable.

She felt the exquisite touch of his hands reaching under her dress, pulling at her knickers as she wrestled frantically with his trousers. Their lips came together with a fierce hunger, their bodies uniting in a frenzied mix of desperate urgency and deep passion, taking them to the magical place that destiny had always intended they should go.

TWENTY-FOUR

They sat on the stairs as their breathing slowly returned to normal, Daniel one step below Abby with his head resting on her lap, her fingers running gently through his hair. 'That was incredible,' he murmured.

'Wonderful,' she said, her tears close to the surface.

He lifted up his head, and their lips came together for a gentle kiss. She put her arms around him as he nestled against her chest.

They stayed in blissful contentment for a few more minutes, until Abby whispered that it was time for them to move.

Daniel got to his feet and began to pull up his trousers. But Abby stopped him. 'No, don't do that. I want to see you naked.'

'Anything you say,' he grinned, kicking off his shoes, stepping out of his trousers, then removing the remainder of his clothes and throwing them in the direction of the hall bench.

'You're so beautiful,' she said, her eyes wandering over every inch of him. Then she stretched out her legs towards him. 'Now it's my turn.'

He took his time, carefully removing her shoes and placing them side by side on the floor. His hands reached under her dress once again, searching for the tops of her stockings, his eyes never leaving hers. He heard her catch her breath as his fingertips delicately caressed her thighs, slowly rolling her stockings down one by one.

Then he took hold of her hand and helped her up. As she stood on the bottom step, he watched her untie the strap of her dress. Watched, mesmerised, as she let the dress fall to her feet.

The sight of her naked in front of him was exhilarating. He took a step forward, his hands exploring the softness of her skin, his tongue gently teasing her nipples.

'Stay with me tonight,' he whispered as his mouth made its way up to her lips.

'Yes,' she said without hesitation. She knew she was breaking her own rules, but at that precise moment she didn't care. Her feelings for him eclipsed everything else. There had never been anyone like Daniel. No-one else had kissed her or touched her or loved her with such intense passion.

He wrapped his arms around her hips and lifted her off the step. Keeping her feet off the floor, he walked to his room, holding her tightly against him, and they fell onto the bed together.

'Are you happy?' he asked, covering her face and neck with tiny kisses.

'I feel glorious,' she beamed.

'Your Quality Quivers were amazing,' he said, his mouth

moving down to her breasts.

'You noticed,' she giggled.

'Of course I noticed. It felt fantastic.' He rolled onto his side, taking her with him. 'Now, what R's do you have for me?' he grinned, his fingers playing between her legs.

Despite the distractions, or perhaps because of them, she had no trouble finding the words she was looking for. 'Ravenously Randy,' she smiled.

'That's exactly what I am,' he laughed. Then he kissed her tenderly. 'Do you want to go again?'

'What do you think,' she said softly, reaching down to him, her fingers gently stroking.

Her touch was electric. 'My Adorable Abby,' he whispered close to her ear. 'How will I ever get enough of you?'

Abby was the first to wake up. She lay quietly beside Daniel, listening to his gentle breathing, feeling the warm touch of his skin against hers.

Somewhere along the way their flirtatiousness had turned into sexual tension, before exploding into a deeply intense and personal experience so different from anything she had ever felt before. She could never regret it. She would hold the memory close to her heart for the rest of her life.

But she was alarmed at how reckless she had been. At how easily she had broken the rules and allowed herself to be swept along by passion. In doing so she had done the one thing she had always been afraid of. She had put their friendship at risk.

They would have to talk about it, but not in this setting. If she was still here when he woke up, she would just want to do it again and again. She allowed herself a few more precious moments with him before slowly removing herself from his bed. He looked so beautiful as he slept, his lips slightly apart as if he were inviting her to kiss them. She closed her eyes against temptation, turned round and quietly left the room.

Their discarded clothing was scattered on the floor in the hall, poignant reminders of what had happened just a few hours earlier. That incredible first time that she would treasure forever. Her dress was still lying in a heap on the stairs. Feeling vulnerable in her nakedness, she slipped it on. Then she laid Daniel's clothes on the hall bench alongside his jacket, picked up her stockings and pants, and made her way up to her own room.

As she stood under the shower, enjoying the meditative power of the warm water rushing over her, her overriding thought was that she had to remain resolute. They had already gone from one time to one night. If she wasn't careful, one night would turn into one week, then one week into one month. The longer it went on the higher the fall would be when their world collapsed beneath them.

And it would collapse, she was certain of that. She remembered the way his friends had teased him at the barbecue. Could she really expect Daniel to commit himself to her for the rest of his life? As a friend, yes. But not as a loving partner.

She couldn't face breakfast. She had no appetite at all. Out of habit she made a pot of coffee, but had no interest in drinking any. She opened the fridge and poured herself a glass of orange juice, taking small sips as her mind went through what she was going to say to Daniel. How she was going to explain to him that it could never happen again.

Hadn't he always known she was against any romantic relationship between them? Even so, she was nervous about his reaction. Would he assume that things would be different now? That her actions last night were proof that she had changed her mind?

It was all so complicated. She needed to see him desperately, to feel his arms surrounding her. And yet she knew she must try and keep her distance. She had to stay strong.

Daniel walked into the kitchen and found Abby sitting there in her dressing gown. At the sight of her, happiness swept over him. 'Morning, beautiful,' he grinned.

She turned round and gave him a smile. 'Morning.'

He sat down beside her, kissed her lightly on the lips and took hold of her hand. She was powerless to stop the thoughts running through her head as she felt his touch. She wanted to be naked in front of him once again. Wanted to feel his hands and his mouth moving hungrily over every inch of her body.

'I missed my Scrumptious Solicitor,' he said. 'You should have woken me up.'

'I took a shower. And you looked so peaceful. I didn't want to disturb you.'

She went over to the coffee machine and filled two mugs, needing something to distract her. But he came up behind her, wrapping his arms around her waist, his warm breath on her cheek. 'Do you have some words for me?'

'My Tasty Temptation,' she said after just a moment's hesitation.

But there was a calmness to her voice that worried him. She wasn't showing the same elation that he was feeling. The overwhelming emotion of true love. 'You don't regret it do you?' he asked quietly.

'No, never. It was wonderful.'

Her words reassured him. 'It certainly was,' he said. 'What was in that champagne?' But the joke fell flat, and he instantly regretted it. 'I'm sorry, that was a ridiculous thing to say. I'm just so crazy in love with you, I'm losing control.' He pushed her hair to one side and began to kiss her on her neck. Small delicate kisses that sent her mind into turmoil, her heart into longing.

How on earth was she going to tell him? Was it even the right thing to do?

'It was the best sex I've ever had,' he murmured between kisses, and he felt her flinch at his words. He knew at once that he had said the wrong thing again, but this time there was more he wanted to say. 'Let me explain,' he started, but she shut him down.

'No, Daniel. There's something I need to say.' She had to say it, however difficult it was going to be, although the things he had said would make the task slightly easier. If he could joke about it, if he thought of it as just sex, maybe he wouldn't take it as badly as she had first thought.

His arms dropped to his sides as she turned to face him. 'I do love you,' she said. 'And I love what we did last night. I will never regret it and never forget it.'

He steeled himself for what he knew was coming next. The 'but' that she had left hanging in the air. The 'but' that she was going to use to smash his hopes and shatter his heart.

'But it has to be just that one night. It will be a beautiful, happy memory. Something wonderful between friends.'

'We are so much more to each other than that, Abby.'

'What we have together is amazing, but we have to stay just friends.'

'What if it's already too late for that?' he said, the anger in his voice unmistakeable.

She knew he didn't mean it. He couldn't mean it. 'Don't you think this is hurting me, too?'

'Maybe it is. But you have the power to do something about it. Whereas I just have to accept everything you say.'

'Daniel, that's not fair. You've always known how I've felt. I've always said I wanted us to stay just friends.'

Her voice began to tremble, her eyes glistening with unshed tears. He couldn't bear to see her upset and took her in his arms. 'I haven't forgotten my promise to you, Abby, and I stand by it. I'll stand by it for the rest of my life. You'll never be without me.'

'Thank you for understanding.'

'I didn't say I understood. But we'll figure it out.'

'Yes, we will.' She gave him a nervous smile. 'And now I think I should go and get dressed.'

His eyes followed her as she walked out into the hall, noticing how incredibly sexy she looked even in her shapeless dressing gown. Or perhaps that was because he knew what was underneath. The image came unbidden into his mind of her dress dropping down to her ankles. It wasn't helping.

He took his coffee and went out onto the balcony. Life carried on as usual down below. People going about their business as if it were just another day. But nothing was the same in his world. How had it gone so wrong?

Abby suddenly appeared beside him, her shoeless feet making no sound on the wooden floor. 'I thought I'd pop into the office. I won't be long.'

He stood up to face her. 'So now you're running away?'

'I did tell you I'd be going in sometime this week. And I thought it would be better if we both had some alone time.'

'Whatever you say.'

'Please don't be like this, Daniel.'

'Come on, Abby, I have to deal with it in my own way. I can't be as calm and accepting as you are.'

'I'm sorry. I'll see you later.'

He turned away from her, her words making it abundantly clear that he wasn't being invited to join her on the walk to work.

But there was no way she could leave without a proper goodbye. She took hold of his hand, and he turned back towards her. 'Bye, then,' she said.

He sighed, but gave her what she wanted. 'Bye, Abby.'

They stared at each other, so many unsaid words hanging between them. Neither of them having a clue how they could come back from this when their wishes seemed so far apart.

TWENTY-FIVE

Abby turned round when she reached the middle of the bridge, hoping to see Daniel on the balcony. But it was empty. She realised there was no way she could face the office today, not in her state of mind. No-one was expecting her, anyway. There was no real reason for her to go in. Perhaps Daniel had been right. She was running away.

It was too soon to go back home, so she crossed the road and walked down the embankment towards Adam's bench. But she was alarmed to see there was someone sitting on it. She kept walking, not wanting to stop and chat. Not wanting to sit on any of the other benches.

Further along there was a riverside café where she stopped for a coffee. Something to fill time before going home. It was a popular place, and she chose to sit at a quiet table outside, away from the intrusive chatter of other customers.

As she sipped her latte, Abby played out in her mind what would happen next between herself and Daniel. They would talk things through and agree to put last night behind them. They would have a weekend in London to visit his friends. They would have their Thanksgiving dinner. Then Daniel would return to Canada as planned, and she would join him in December for a holiday.

If she received a positive response to her application – and there was no reason to suppose otherwise – she would be starting her therapy course in January. A new chapter in her life that would add to her skill set and bring new opportunities.

Her relationship with Daniel would go back to how it had always been: a warm and loving friendship. Perhaps when enough time had passed they would be able to talk fondly about what had happened between them.

Of course, the solution was only that simple once emotions had been taken out of the equation. The reality was likely to be very different. But she wouldn't allow herself to think about that.

When Abby arrived back home, Daniel was on the phone. He heard her come in and came into the hall from the kitchen, tapping his thumb and fingers together and rolling his eyes. She guessed correctly that he was talking to Paula. It was about seven in the morning in Toronto. What was so urgent? She gave him a sympathetic smile, then went into the kitchen as he went into his room.

She put her bag down on the island, but her eyes were drawn to Daniel's open laptop on the dining table. He had always said he was happy for her to read his drafts, so she had no hesitation in looking at what he had written that morning. It was the sex scene between the two detectives that they had discussed the week after his arrival. She knew he had decided against using the scenario they had enacted together, and the difficulties he'd had in coming up with an alternative.

Almost immediately she became uneasy at what she was reading. What had been fun and romantic had now been rewritten into something dark and desperate. And yet there were undeniable similarities with their own experience the night before. The stumbling onto the stairs, the fierce intensity of the kiss, the frantic undressing. It was all there.

Even though she knew there was a high chance that the pain she was feeling would increase, she kept reading. It was impossible to stop. She needed to know everything he had written.

Then she came to one line that she could not get past: *For him, it was an act of pure physical need and nothing more; his touch totally bereft of any tenderness or affection.*

She felt numb. Was this a true account of Daniel's experience? But she had been there, too. She had felt the passion and the desire mixed with the need. The love that had overwhelmed the lust. She stared at the page, trying to make sense of the words she was seeing. A terrible thought suddenly found its way into her head. Had he been acting out another scene for his book?

If she had been given more time to think about it rationally, she would have coped much better. She would have been calm enough to discuss it with him objectively. Calm enough to listen to his point of view.

But when Daniel suddenly appeared in front of her, her

emotions were still raw. She had no control over the words that came tumbling out of her mouth. Words that shocked them both.

'So when exactly did you start to realise it would make a good addition to your story, Daniel? When we were falling onto the stairs? When you were pressing your lips hard against mine? When you were pulling off my knickers?'

He stared at her, a look of incredulity on his face. He had seen her with his laptop. He knew what she must have read. But he had not been expecting such a hostile reaction. 'Seriously, Abby? You're unbelievable.'

'Well, what am I supposed to think after what I've just read?'

'For pity's sake, they're characters in a fictional story. They're not you and I. You know that.'

'But so much of what you've written actually happened. We've completely merged with those characters. How can I separate the truth from your imagination?'

He knew she was hurting, knew he needed to put things right. They had been shouting back and forth, but his next words were softer. He was desperate to get her on side. 'Because you know me. Because you know I would never think of you in that way.'

Her anger was still smouldering, and she gave him an icy stare. 'And yet you told me this morning that you'd seen it all through your champagne goggles. How do you think that made me feel?'

'Don't put words in my mouth,' he said, exasperated with her. 'I never said that at all.'

'You said something about the champagne having an effect.'

He sighed deeply, but kept his voice calm. 'I'm not going to argue anymore, Abby. I'll delete the whole scene, if that's what you want.'

'Oh, do what you like,' she snapped, turning round and retreating to her room, determined not to cry in front of him.

As she flopped down on the bed her tears began to fall. But she was more upset with herself than she was with Daniel. Why had she handled the situation so badly? Once she had composed herself, she would go and talk to him. Apologise for the things she had said.

Daniel closed his laptop with more force than he intended, angry at what had unfolded between himself and Abby. He tidied up his papers and took them into his room, along with the laptop that had sparked their argument. It had always been his intention to talk to her about what he had written and ask her opinion. He would never have used it without her agreement. Surely she should have known that?

There was really only one choice left to him. He refused to wait for her to calm down. First he'd had to deal with the pain of her rejection, and now her astonishing suggestion that he had been acting out a scene for his novel. It was too much. He'd had enough.

When he re-emerged from his bedroom, he soon realised Abby was still upstairs. He called up to her from the hallway. 'I'm leaving now, Abby. I'm checking back into the hotel.'

He waited for her at the foot of the stairs. She came out of her room and sat down on the top step, her eyes bright with tears. But he resisted the urge to take her in his arms and comfort her. It seemed pointless at this late stage. It would change nothing.

Her eyes became focused on his suitcase and what it meant. Of all the things he could have told her, she had not been expecting him to say he was leaving. 'You don't have to do this,' she said, her voice unsteady.

'Actually, I do.'

'Daniel, I'm so sorry I reacted the way I did. Of course I know you weren't acting out a scene last night. I know it was real. It was just hard seeing those words in black and white.'

'Yes, I can understand that. But the problem is you've twisted things so that I'm suddenly the bad guy. You've made it all about you, and yet I'm the one who's been rejected. You seem to have forgotten that.'

'I'm just trying to protect our friendship.'

'Maybe that's what you think you're doing, but you're going about it the wrong way. Making love with you was fantastic. Incredible. Now you've tainted that experience for me.'

As he turned towards the door Abby ran down the stairs to join him. 'No, please don't say that. It *was* incredible. Stay and talk about it.'

'Why? Do you think I can convince you to change your

mind?'

She looked down at the floor and shook her head.

'Then there's no point in me staying,' he said. 'Weren't you the one who said we needed some alone time?'

'I didn't mean you should leave.'

'Maybe not, but that's my decision.'

'You'll stay in touch? You'll let me know what you're doing?'

'I'll text you when I've got something to say.'

'Daniel, please don't go.'

'Bye, Abby.'

She stared at the door as it shut behind him. She could hear the ping signalling the arrival of the lift. Hear the sound of the doors opening and closing. Taking him away from her.

Hadn't she always known this would be the outcome if they went too far with their relationship? But none of that mattered anymore. There was no joy or satisfaction to be had in being right.

TWENTY-SIX

Daniel made use of the hotel pool, then spent the remainder of the day up in his room immersed in his writing. He ordered a light meal in the evening before phoning Matt to arrange a visit down to London. They agreed that Daniel would arrive Friday evening and stay until the following Monday.

'No, Abby won't be coming with me,' he said in reply to Matt's query.

'Really? She seemed very keen when I spoke to her Saturday night.'

'That's Abby for you. Very keen one minute, loses interest the next.'

'What's happened, mate?'

'It's a bloody nightmare. We slept together last night, then this morning she couldn't get out of bed fast enough. We had a stupid row, and now I'm back in the hotel.'

'What went wrong? Was it a drunken night that she regrets?'

'Not at all. The problem is she's got herself into this mindset where she's convinced she has to keep us in the friend zone.'

'And you want more than that?'

'Yeah, I do. To be honest, I'm crazy about her. I'd marry her tomorrow if she'd have me. But there's no chance of that.'

'If you'd rather get yourself away from there, you're welcome to come up to London before Friday. We'll be working, but you can stay at the flat.'

'Thanks, but I'll pass. I'll be focused on writing over the next few days. My agent's chasing me for chapters.'

'A bit of a romance novel this time?'

'Very funny! Clearly I'm pretty hopeless at romance. Just ask Abby.' But he wondered if he had confided too much in Matt. How would Abby feel if she found out? 'Listen mate, you won't pass any of this on, will you? If it gets back to Abby that people are talking about her, things could escalate.'

'I would love to see you two together. I wouldn't do anything to mess that up,' Matt assured him.

Abby was also keeping herself busy that afternoon. She changed the bedlinen in Daniel's room, refusing to let her emotions get the better of her as she did so. But she was unable to stop the memories flooding back. Was it really only last night?

She had no idea when she would be seeing Daniel again, but she thought it best to wait for Daniel to contact her. He would have to come back to the flat to pick up the rest of his belongings. Then they could talk things through calmly and rationally. At least make an attempt to mend the rift between them. Yes, he had said he would keep his promise to her and always be in her life. But she would never forgive herself if they lost their deep connection. If their close bond became fractured.

There was no-one else she wanted to talk to about it. No-one else she wanted to see. Only Daniel. She stayed up late into the night until she fell asleep in front of the TV, waking up as the credits rolled on a film she couldn't remember watching. Then she took herself to bed.

The next morning she was relieved to receive his text, although the words were not what she would have wished for: *FYI I'll be going to London on Friday and staying with Matt. I'd like to come over to collect more of my stuff before then.*

Clearly he was still angry with her. Nothing was said about her accompanying him to London, but his silence on that point told her he would be going alone. Pushing that aside, she focused on the fact that he would be coming over and replied straightaway: *Of course. I'll see you soon.*

She stayed away from the office over the next couple of days. It seemed unlikely that Daniel would let himself in unannounced, but after the way he had left she couldn't be certain what he would do. It was essential that she was at home when he came over. Then they could have the conversation that was so desperately needed.

On Wednesday lunchtime, Abby received an unexpected call from Georgia. 'I heard some very interesting news this morning from one of my yoga friends,' she said. 'And I'm a bit worried about you.'

'I'm fine,' Abby said. 'What on earth have you heard?'

'Michelle works at The Waterfront. Apparently, a certain Mr Stratton checked back in on Monday.'

'I would have thought staff members should be keeping details about their hotel customers confidential,' Abby said frostily.

'Obviously. But she knows I was at his party at the weekend. It was a private chat, not a public announcement.'

'Whatever it was, it's not news to me. Daniel finds it easier to concentrate on his writing when I'm not around. He's moved back into the hotel for a few days.'

'Abby, contrary to public opinion, I'm not completely stupid. You sound upset. What's happened?'

'Georgia, please don't read anything into it. I'm fine. Honestly.'

'But you clearly need cheering up, so we'll be having an impromptu girls' night at your place. I'll bring the wine. You order the pizza. We'll be there at seven.'

'You haven't even asked me if I'm doing anything tonight.'

'And are you?'

'Well, no.'

'Of course not. We'll see you later.' And with that, Georgia hung up.

Abby had been given no real opportunity to object, but she hadn't spoken to any of her friends since the party and was grateful to Georgia for her intervention. Remembering the dreary evening she had spent on her own yesterday, a girls' night in could be was just what she needed. She phoned Luca's and ordered a large pizza and some gelato for seven fifteen.

Georgia was first through the door and gave Abby a hug before disappearing into the kitchen with the wine to look for a corkscrew and glasses. 'Thanks for coming,' Abby said to Asha and Ellie. 'It's so good to see you.'

'Georgia said you needed cheering up,' Asha said. 'She's worried about you.'

'I'm fine. Just a bit lonely now Daniel's moved back into the hotel.' Then she laughed at herself. 'And I know how stupid that sounds when I've been living on my own for years.'

'It sounds as if you've enjoyed having him around,' Ellie said. 'Of course you're going to miss him.'

They all moved into the kitchen, where Georgia was pouring out the wine. 'Have you ordered pizza?' she asked.

'Yes. From Luca's. Goat's cheese and fig.'

'Lovely. And is the delicious Marco delivering it for us?'

'I doubt it. He's not often there these days. And even if he was, I hardly think he'd be doing the deliveries.'

'I seem to remember a time when he did rather a lot for you.'

'Yes, well, that was a long time ago. I wish you would stop bringing it up.'

'She's just jealous because she didn't manage to snare him for herself, despite her best efforts,' Ellie smiled.

Georgia shrugged. 'It's his loss.' Then she moved on to

another topic Abby could have done without. 'Are you going to be in London this weekend?' she asked.

Abby hesitated before giving her reply, then kept it short. 'No, I'm not.' The sound of the buzzer was a welcome distraction. There would be no need for her to expand on her answer.

But whilst they were enjoying the pizza, Georgia carried on with the conversation. 'I was thinking of going down to London myself,' she said. 'But if you're not going, that changes things. I expect they're planning a boys-only weekend.'

'Yes, probably, 'Abby said. 'How are things with Troy?' she added, keen to stop anyone focusing on herself and Daniel.

'Oh, don't get her started on Troy again,' Asha laughed. 'He was all she talked about in the car.'

'Troy is fabulous,' Georgia said. 'But Liam wants me to go to a party with him on Saturday. I was unsure which one to choose, but you've made my mind up for me.'

'So you're going to finish with Troy?' Ellie asked.

'Did I say that?' Georgia laughed. 'We're not exclusive. I'm sure I'll be seeing him again sooner or later.'

'You live in a different world,' Asha smiled. 'Can you ever see yourself settling down?'

'Settling down is not in my vocabulary,' Georgia said. 'And it'll be great to see Liam again. It's always so good getting back together after we've had a break.'

'You'll still be playing with men's hearts in the nursing home in fifty years' time,' Ellie smiled.

Their laughter almost drowned out another push of the door buzzer. But Abby had heard it. She hurried into the hall.

'Hello?'

'It's me. Just checking if it's convenient for you.'

'Daniel, of course it is. I'd love to see you.'

But he could hear the sound of laughter coming from the kitchen. 'Are you having a party?' he asked.

'The girls came over to cheer me up.' As soon as she said the words she wished she could take them back.

'Then I'll leave you to it.'

'No, come on up. Please.' She pressed the button, but Daniel ignored the click of the door unlocking.

'Not tonight. Another time.'

It had been a mistake to come. He retraced his steps, his hands in his pockets, his head bowed, wondering what story Abby had spun to her girlfriends that would show him in a bad light. Or had they been enjoying the fact that it was a man being made a fool of rather than one of them?

But the negative thoughts that swept through his mind were only a hopeless attempt to turn himself against her. He knew those thoughts were not a true reflection of who she was. He wasn't ready to give up on her, but right now he needed a distraction.

He turned into the pub just before the bridge, not wanting to spend another lonely night in his hotel room. There were three men playing pool, and they were happy for him to join them. They were not interested in his history or his reasons for being in England. He was just Daniel, a visitor from Canada who was staying at The Waterfront. He spent an enjoyable evening in good company, temporarily relegating his problems to the back of his mind.

TWENTY-SEVEN

As Daniel stepped out of the shower the following morning, a text arrived from Abby: *Sorry about last night. I'm here all day. Come over any time.*

His heart told him to get over there as soon as possible, his head told him to take his time. He read the text again. There was nothing to indicate she was eager to see him. So he chose the latter, not willing to make a fool of himself yet again.

Three hours later he was at her door. Her voice and her smile told him she was happy to see him, but he was careful not to let his guard down. He accepted her offer of a coffee. 'How was girls' night?' he asked.

'It was good, thanks. Pizza and wine and a lot of talking.'

'And was my atrocious behaviour the reason you needed cheering up?'

'Daniel, please don't. You're not to blame for anything. Georgia heard from a friend that you had checked into the hotel. That's all it was. She was worried about me.'

'And was she right to be worried about you?'

'Not really, I'm fine.'

'I'm glad to hear it,' he said, with no attempt to hide the sarcasm in his voice. Seeing her again had only amplified the pain of her rejection. 'It certainly sounded as if you were enjoying yourselves,' he continued. 'Having a good laugh at my expense, no doubt.'

'Of course not. I didn't tell them anything about what we did. But I do want to talk to you about it. We can't go on like this.'

'I don't see how we can resolve anything when you're so bloody adamant that your way is the only way. When you refuse to give us a chance.'

There was nothing new she could think of to say. She sipped her coffee and tried to remember the conversation she had imagined they would be having, but nothing seemed to fit the scenario they now found themselves in.

'I'll go and pack my stuff,' Daniel said, leaving her alone in the kitchen.

When she heard his bedroom door opening, followed by the sound of a suitcase trundling across the floor, she came out of the kitchen and leant against the wall. 'Can you stay for lunch?' she asked.

He turned to face her, his body only inches away from hers. 'I'm hungry for you, Abby. Nothing else. I could eat you up.'

His words rendered her speechless. She froze, alarmed at the thoughts she couldn't control, scared of what she might do if she took just half a step towards him.

He put his hands on the wall either side of her, careful not to touch her, then moved his head closer and began to whisper in her ear. 'What if I brush my lips against yours? What if I gently caress your tongue with mine? What if I stroke my hand delicately up your inner thigh? Will I feel how much you want me right now?'

'Daniel, stop!'

He instantly stepped away from her. 'Now *that* is what you should have told me on Sunday night. Have you any idea how much you hurt me, playing games like you did? It wasn't just a one-night stand for me. I told you I was in love with you. You knew I wanted a relationship. At no point did you tell me you weren't feeling the same. You must have realised you were making me believe we had a future together. It was a cruel way to treat your best friend.'

She could feel her eyes filling with tears and willed them not to fall. 'Daniel, please forgive me. I'm so sorry for the pain I've caused you. But it wasn't a game. I wanted you so much. I've never denied that. You know how much I love you.'

'But it's not enough, is it?'

'I honestly never meant to hurt you.'

'Is that right? Don't worry about it. I'm pretty sure I'll be able to find someone in London who won't be in such a hurry to leave my bed.'

His words hit a nerve, as they were intended to, but she did her best not to show it. 'If the opportunity arises, then do it. I've got no hold on you.'

'Oh yes you have, Abby. You know you have.'

'You're free to sleep with whoever you want. It's

nothing to do with me.'

'And what if I only want to sleep with you?'

'It can't happen again, Daniel. I've told you that.'

'Yes, you've told me. But it makes no sense.'

'Maybe not now, but one day it will. I know it will. We're so good together as friends. We need to hold on to that.'

He scoffed at her words. 'Oh Abby, we could have so much more. I want you to think seriously about everything we've meant to each other. Everything you're carelessly throwing away. Then come and tell me we're nothing more than friends.'

He turned round when he reached the front door. 'I'll see you next week.'

'Have a good weekend,' she said, struggling to keep her voice calm.

'I certainly hope so.'

She watched the door shut behind him, knowing how close she had come to breaking the rules once again. Was it going to be like this every time she saw him?

Her tears began to fall, and she hastily wiped them away. If she wanted to keep her best friend, she had to stay strong.

TWENTY-EIGHT

With Daniel on his way to London, Abby finally made a visit to the office. She managed to avoid her colleagues. The last thing she needed was a debrief about her time off. Specifically the weekend.

But Abby was happy to chat about it with Emily. When they were settled in her office, she gave Emily a succinct account of the weekend. Nothing too personal, just the facts.

'I found some photos online,' Emily said. She took out her phone and showed Abby one of the pictures that Georgia had posted. 'Is this Daniel's girlfriend?' she asked.

'No, that's my friend Georgia. They met for the first time at the party. That's one of the photos I took.'

Abby read the caption underneath: *Me with bestselling author Daniel Stratton at his party last night. Who knew a writer could be so delicious?*

She knew. She had always known. Wasn't he her Daniel Delicious? Only he wasn't hers anymore, was he? She had pushed him away.

'Is he coming to pick you up today?' Emily asked, jolting Abby out of her thoughts.

'No, he's in London for the weekend. I'm afraid you won't be seeing him again before he goes back to Canada.'

'Oh, that's a pity.'

'I know, but he has less than two weeks left and a lot to fit in.' How much longer could she keep up the charade? She quickly moved on. 'It's time I did some work. What have you got for me?'

They spent the next half an hour going through the post, and discussing phone calls and emails that had been received during Abby's absence. 'Can you carry on as if I'm not here?' she asked before Emily went back to her desk. 'No calls or interruptions.'

'Yes, of course.'

Abby answered a few emails, made a couple of phone calls and updated her schedule. After two hours she had done all she could, and made her way back to her empty flat.

Later that afternoon she received a positive reply about the therapy course. She desperately wanted to share her news with Daniel. But that would have to wait.

Abby had told her mother there was a high chance she would be going to London at the weekend. As she hadn't been told anything to the contrary, Beth wasn't expecting to see Abby on Saturday. But after Abby's last two meetings with Daniel had gone so badly, she felt a strong need to open up to her mother. It was impossible to explain everything over the phone, so she took a chance that Beth would be home.

But her driving was too fast for the twists and turns of the country roads. As she came round a bend, she drifted over to the wrong side. The frantic beeping from an oncoming car gave her just enough time to avoid a collision.

She pulled over at a convenient spot about a hundred yards further on, her body still shaking. Her first instinct was to call Daniel. But she wasn't hurt. There was no legitimate reason to interrupt his weekend. She called Beth's landline instead. If she didn't answer, she would turn round and drive slowly and carefully back home.

But Beth did answer and, in spite of Abby's attempts to keep control of her voice, knew straightaway that something was wrong. 'What's happened, sweetheart? Are you okay?'

'Not really. Can I come over?'

'Of course you can. I'm here all day.'

'I'm only five minutes away. I just wanted to check you were in.'

When she arrived at Beth's front door, Beth wrapped her arms around her, took her into the kitchen and made her a cup of tea.

'I've messed everything up, Mum,' Abby said through her tears. 'Daniel hates me.'

'I find that very hard to believe. Why don't you tell me what's happened.'

She dried her tears and took a deep breath before telling Beth the basics. 'We had an amazing weekend away. Then Daniel took me to Castaways on Sunday night, and we ended up sleeping together. Now he says he wants a relationship, even though I've always said that can never happen. I can't make him understand. He moved back into the hotel on Monday, and yesterday he went off to London without me.'

'He'll be hurting, Abby. Leave him to come to terms with it on his own. Give him time.'

'But I can't lose him, Mum.'

'You won't lose him. Daniel would never break his promise to you.'

'That's what he said. But things have already changed between us. We can't talk to each other like we used to. We're always arguing.'

'What did you expect would happen, Abby?'

'I know. I was stupid and naïve. But I love him, Mum. I just wanted to know what it would be like to be with him.' She paused, the tears threatening to return. Beth took hold of her hand and waited patiently for her to carry on.

'And it was wonderful,' Abby said softly, her mind full of images of their night together. 'But if we try to have a relationship, it wouldn't last. It would burn out just like my marriage, and we'd be left with nothing.'

'Not all relationships end like that, Abby. But if you feel you don't love him enough, then you really have to tell him.'

'No, it's not that at all. I love him so much. More than I loved Gavin. But I can see him getting bored with me just like Gavin did.'

'Why would you say that?'

'Because the morning after, he made a joke about it. Then he said it was the best sex he'd ever had, as if it were just sex. And you know he's never been interested in long-term relationships.'

'Perhaps because he hasn't found someone who matches up to you.'

'Do you really think that?'

'I think he loves you more than you know, Abby. And the joking is just part of who he is. I'm certain he would never deliberately say something to offend you.'

'You think I'm being unkind? Daniel said I was cruel. I don't like who I've become. I'm such a horrible person.'

'No you're not. Please don't say things like that. You and Daniel are two people in love who are trying to deal with their feelings. You mustn't dwell on the hurtful things you've said to one another. Why don't you make a fresh start when you see each other again and go from there?'

'We can try.'

'And I'm always here for you, Abby. Talk to me, don't bottle things up.'

'Thanks, Mum,' she said, laying her head on Beth's shoulder, relieved that she had finally opened up about her love for Daniel.

At half past six on Sunday morning, Abby was sitting on the balcony in her dressing gown, wrapped in a cosy throw to combat the chill. A mist lay over the town, and in the east a streak of orange and turquoise sky sat between the shadows of the trees and the thin dark clouds. It was a beautiful sight. Something she wished she could have been sharing with Daniel. She missed him so much.

Today would be another pyjama Sunday, although this time there would be no chance that Daniel would make a surprise appearance. He was not due back from London until sometime on Monday. How long he would stay at the hotel before contacting her, she had no idea.

If only she had done things differently. Stopped to think before starting an argument with him. She had treated him so badly. What was it that had changed her from a caring, confident and organised woman into a mass of selfishness, indecisions and inconsistencies? It could only be love.

Love. All those powerful emotions that are so hard to handle, that make ordinary people behave totally out of character. It was those emotions that were tearing them apart, making it impossible for them to have a calm and rational conversation. What if she tried another approach?

She spent the afternoon on her laptop, attempting to put her thoughts into some kind of cohesive order. The next step was going to be either emailing Daniel or writing him a letter that she could drop off at the hotel.

But as she read through her draft, she began to change her mind. It was far too long and unwieldy. A neat and concise two-line email sounded a much better option. Nothing more than a request to meet up somewhere neutral.

She finally came up with something she was happy with: *I'm so sorry for hurting you, Daniel. I miss you. I'll be on*

Dad's bench at half eight tomorrow morning. I would love to meet you there, Abby x

Perhaps Adam's bench could not really be classed as neutral, but it was a place where they both felt comfortable. They could use it as the starting point for a walk by the river, maybe stopping for breakfast in the nearby café, then finally have the talk they had both been avoiding.

She saved the email in her draft folder and left it unsent until the following day.

TWENTY-NINE

At six o'clock on Monday evening, Abby finally pressed the send button. She was astonished when a reply came back within seconds: *I'll be there. Check your post box. Great minds… x*

Daniel had left something in her post box? She couldn't get downstairs fast enough. There was an envelope waiting for her that had obviously been hand delivered. A cream envelope with the hotel's name and logo on it. She took it back up to the flat, staring at her name in Daniel's distinctive writing, both intrigued and nervous as to what she might find inside.

The envelope stayed in her hand, unopened, until she was sitting on the snuggle chair in her bedroom. Then she opened it carefully and removed the letter, written on a page torn from Daniel's notebook: *To my AA, forgive me for the hurtful things I said and for leaving when I should have stayed. Being crazy in love has transformed me into an irrational fool. Forever yours, DD x*

Her eyes filled with tears as she held the letter close to her heart. She quickly messaged a reply: *Until tomorrow x*

There was no suggestion that they meet up that

evening. After being apart for a week, she was well aware that getting back together at the end of the day would come with the additional complication of heightened emotions. Reading his letter had brought tears to her eyes. She was in no fit state to meet him face-to-face.

Abby was up before her alarm the next morning. She was so eager to see Daniel again, even half past eight seemed ridiculously late. It was still three hours away.

She wondered whether or not he would be ready to come back to the flat. It was what she wanted, but she was nervous about asking him. She didn't want to get his hopes up, that would be too unkind. Hadn't she hurt him enough already?

Despite taking her time getting dressed, she was ready far too early. By quarter to eight she couldn't wait any longer and started her walk. She took the longer route rather than going over the road bridge, walking along the other side of the river and down to the footbridge, then approaching the benches from the other direction.

As she stepped off the bridge, she could see there was someone sitting on Adam's bench again. But this time it made her smile. It was someone very familiar. Someone who was looking in the other direction and hadn't noticed her. Suddenly he turned in her direction and immediately stood up. She increased her pace.

'Hey, gorgeous,' he grinned. 'What are you doing here so early?'

'What about you?' she laughed. 'It's becoming a habit.'

'A bad one?'

'No, it's definitely good,' she said, kissing him lightly on the cheek. 'I'm so happy to see you.'

They sat down together, their thighs touching, his arm loosely across her shoulders. 'Have you had breakfast?' he asked. 'I thought we could go back to the hotel and eat there.'

'Yes, I'd like that. But can we talk here first? It'll be quieter than the hotel.'

'Of course.'

'When did you come over with the letter?'

'About four o'clock. I didn't know if you'd be at work or not.'

'I was home. I decided not to keep messing them about with my days off. Why didn't you buzz?'

'After the way I left, I couldn't be sure of your reaction. It was a huge relief when I saw your email.'

'Do you think we're ready to have a conversation without it turning into another row?'

'Who knows? When emotions are involved, anything can happen. But I would like to know why making love with me didn't change your opinion of us. Did you think I wasn't serious?'

'I suppose the things you said made it easier to say what I had to say. But I was never going to change my mind. I'm so sorry, Daniel, but I still can't.'

'What things? You mean that stupid champagne joke?'

'A little bit, but mostly it was you saying it was the best sex of your life. As if it were just sex and nothing more than that.'

He gave a sigh and shook his head. Yes, he had told her it had been the best sex of his life, but that hadn't been the end of his thoughts. He would have said a lot more if she hadn't given him the impression she didn't want to talk about it. He had gone along with that rather than reveal the true extent of his feelings, which had clearly been the wrong thing to do. There was no way he was going to repeat his mistake.

'I did say that, and I meant it. But your interpretation couldn't be further from the truth. I would have told you more if you hadn't cut me off.'

'I won't do that again, Daniel. I want to hear everything you have to say.'

'It *was* the best sex of my life, because for the first time I was having sex with someone who I'm deeply in love with. I was truly making love. The intensity of it and the passion was off the scale. It was an incredible experience. One I've only ever shared with you.'

She took hold of his hand. 'You've just described everything I was feeling. Being with you was amazing. I loved every second of it, because I love you.' Then she hesitated, turning away from him before adding, 'Probably too much.'

'Too much?' His fingers gently turned her face back towards him. 'How can it possibly be too much?'

'Because it's already changed things between us. We've had rows. It's messed up our friendship. And it's bound to make it difficult for us to have other relationships.'

‘Do you want other relationships?’

‘There’s no future in a relationship for us,’ she said automatically.

‘What is it you want, Abby? To spend the next ten years flitting from one guy to the next, never finding the one who makes you truly happy? Stop searching. It always comes back to us. Always. Can’t you see that?’

‘So you want me to believe that I’m so amazing you’d be happy to have no-one else but me for the rest of your life?’

‘Yes, I want you to believe it,’ he laughed. ‘Because you are. Of course you are. Why do you keep doubting me? Why do you keep doubting yourself? It’s crazy.’

‘I won’t risk our friendship, Daniel. However much I love you, I can’t do that.’

‘We wouldn’t be risking anything. Our bond is so strong, there’s no way we would break up.’

‘You don’t know that.’

‘Actually, I do know that.’ He detected an almost imperceptible shake of her head. ‘All right. If for some unfathomable reason we did break up, what you’ve been imagining would never happen. We’ve loved each other for years. We’ve been best friends forever. That won’t change. We will never lose that.’

She refused to look at him, her eyes staring out across the water.

‘It’s really not as complicated as you’re making it, Abby,’ he said softly. ‘Honestly, it isn’t.’

This time she shook her head with more force. ‘No,

Daniel, we need to return to our separate lives to find out for certain what we both want.'

'I already know what I want.'

'Have you even considered that when you're back in Canada you'll feel differently? You might look at our time together as just an enjoyable fling.'

'Abby, that's complete nonsense.'

'That's not fair, Daniel. It's such an important decision. We need to be a hundred per cent certain that it's the right one.'

He made one final attempt to convince her. 'Do you remember how upset you were when I was flirting with the waitress at Luca's?'

'What are you talking about?' she asked, having no idea where he was going.

'Can't you just answer the question?'

'Okay! Yes, I do. But it wasn't the flirting exactly. It was the fact that I felt completely invisible. It was humiliating.'

'I'm so sorry, Abby. That was never my intention. I was in a weird mood that day. It had occurred to me that you might not take me seriously even if I could find the right time to tell you I was in love with you. My mind was in complete chaos. I was attempting to test myself. I wanted to see if I could feel any sort of spark with another woman.'

'And did you?'

He smiled at her. 'No. Absolutely nothing. It was just pointless banter. Then there was the night of my party. You told me it was obvious I didn't want any of the women in my bed.'

'Yes, I remember.'

'Then don't you already have your proof? I'm only interested in you, Abby.'

'I do take you seriously, Daniel. But I still say we need to spend time apart.'

'Then I'll accept that for now,' he said, not wanting to keep pressuring her. If he pushed too far, there was always a danger it would backfire.

'Thank you,' she said.

He rested his forehead on hers. 'Oh, Abby,' he murmured, 'Don't ever doubt how much I love you.' Their lips connected for a gentle kiss. Not the type of kiss he had wanted to give her, but enjoyable nonetheless.

'Are you ready for breakfast?' he asked.

She gave him a warm smile. 'Yes, I think I am.'

'How was your weekend away?' Abby asked as they were sitting in the hotel restaurant.

'It was good. I hope you weren't too upset that I didn't ask you to come with me.'

'No. It made sense after what happened.' She suddenly found herself blushing. 'I mean after our row.'

'I knew what you meant.' Then he smiled at her. 'You look so cute when you blush.'

'Don't! I won't be able to stop if you keep saying things like that.'

'My head is full of things like that about you, Abby,' he grinned. 'I could write a book.'

'Just make sure you get permission first.'

'You know I was always going to do that.'

'Yes, I know. I didn't mean those things I said about your writing.'

'We both said things we didn't mean.' He took hold of her hand. 'We'll figure it out.'

'I hope so.' She poured them both a coffee. 'Did you mention your Thanksgiving party to Matt when you were in London?'

'No, I've decided to give it a miss.' The last thing Daniel needed was to be surrounded by happy couples when Abby was still insisting they had to stay just friends, but he kept that thought to himself.

'Did you tell anyone about us?' she asked, her voice a little shaky.

'I told Matt the day I went back to the hotel. I'm sorry, Abby, but I was so angry. I needed to speak to someone.'

'It's okay. I understand. And he must have kept it quiet, otherwise it would have got back to Georgia.'

'So you didn't tell her?'

'I decided not to. The only person I told was Mum.'

'And what did she say?'

'She said we shouldn't dwell on hurtful things we said to each other. And to give each other time.'

'Beth is a very wise woman,' he smiled.

'She certainly is. And she's invited us both over for dinner on Saturday. She would really love to see you before you leave. Will you come?'

'Definitely. I was hoping I'd get to see her again.'

'That's great. I'll let her know.'

Things were going so well between them that Abby was no longer nervous about asking Daniel her next question. 'You will come back to your room, won't you?' she said in that way she had. Confident that her request would be granted. But this time she had miscalculated.

'No, that's not possible,' he said. It wasn't an invitation to her bed. Nothing had changed. 'I'll be staying at the hotel.'

Her smile faded and turned into a pout. 'I thought we'd be spending your last week together.'

He recognised her attempt to reel him in. But this time it wouldn't be so easy. He couldn't just gloss over her harsh rejection. 'I need to get back to my writing.'

She remembered the call he'd had from Paula before their row. 'Has Paula been chasing you?'

'She has. But it needs tidying up a bit before I send anything to her. Plus I still have to rewrite that sex scene.'

'There's no need to delete what you've written, Daniel. It's a good scene.'

'You don't mind that the inspiration came from what happened with us?'

'No, I'm fine with that. I just wish we could have talked about it before I read it, but that wasn't your fault. I didn't give you a chance.'

'As long as you're sure.'

'I'm sure.' She made one more attempt to win him over. 'Your room's always ready for you, Daniel.'

'It's me who's not ready, Abby.'

'No, I'm sorry. But I'll still see you, won't I?'

Of course he wanted to see her. To be near her. That would never change. 'How about I take you out to dinner tonight?'

'I'd like that,' she said, her smile lighting up her face and warming his heart.

THIRTY

From Abby's viewpoint, they appeared to be moving seamlessly back into friendship mode over the next few days. They would go out for dinner in the evening, a different restaurant each time. Their chat would be flowing but light. Still fun, but the flirting turned down a notch.

Then he would walk her home. There were hugs goodnight outside her front door with a kiss on the cheek. And every morning he would be waiting for her in the lobby, then they would walk to the hotel for a leisurely breakfast.

For Daniel it wasn't that easy. He would spend a few hours in the day perfecting the chapters that his agent was waiting impatiently for, but when he was not working on his novel he was writing a contemporary record of his raw thoughts and emotions about Abby. It was his way of getting through the days and nights without her. He was going along with what she asked of him, but he wanted so much more.

The idea of extending his stay came to him as he was walking back to the hotel on Thursday night.

There was a literary festival he had promised to attend

at the end of October. It might be difficult to persuade Paula to get him out of it, but he could do it. He would be sending her his work the following morning, so she couldn't use that as a reason to object. And there was always the option of attending online. That should be relatively straightforward to arrange.

The challenge would be persuading Abby to alter her mindset and follow her heart.

'I sent my work to Paula before I came out,' Daniel told Abby as they made their way over the bridge the next morning.

'You did? Well done.' At first she hesitated before asking him her question, but what did she have to lose? 'If you don't have any other plans, can we spend the day together?'

'Actually, I do have something planned.'

'Okay, that's fine.' She was disappointed, but made the effort to show an interest. 'What will you be doing?'

'I was thinking about taking a walk on the Downs,' he said. 'And I was hoping you would be joining me.'

'Daniel, don't do that!' She turned to face him. 'We'll have a great time. Thank you so much.'

'You're welcome.' But the urge to kiss her was too strong, and he turned away. 'Come on, we need a good breakfast inside us,' he said, walking swiftly towards the hotel entrance and holding the door open for her.

It was only a thirty-minute drive to the car park on the

Downs. Abby went home to change, then drove her car back to the hotel and picked Daniel up from the hotel car park. The weather was perfect. A clear sky with no rain forecast, and a sunny fourteen degrees.

Just over halfway into the walk they stopped at a pub for a lunch of pie and chips. 'I don't think we'll need a meal out tonight after this,' Abby said.

'No. We can have a quiet night in.'

Was he hinting at something? She couldn't be sure until she noticed a slow smile creeping onto his face. 'Abby, if the offer still stands, I'd like to come back to my room.'

'Tonight?'

'Yes, tonight. If you'd like me to.'

'I'd very much like you to,' she said, her face beaming with happiness.

They walked at a slower pace over the remaining three miles, enjoying each other's company and the spectacular views over the countryside. Their conversation was light, focusing on the present and their surroundings. To Abby, Daniel appeared more like his old self. She managed to convince herself that he had started to come round to her way of thinking.

Once they were back in the car, Abby drove straight to the hotel. They went up to Daniel's room together to pack his things. She was delighted that they wouldn't be back in the morning for breakfast. They would have breakfast in her kitchen once again.

And, before that, they would have a quiet night in. Snuggling up together on the sofa in front of the TV, sipping hot chocolate. A perfect end to a perfect day.

As he lay in bed that night, Daniel was finding it difficult to drift off. All he could think about was what he had been doing with Abby the last time he had been in that bed. In a complete change from the desperate longing of their first time together, the second time had been much slower. A gentle exploration of every part of each other.

He could still remember how she had looked and felt and tasted. How they had clung to each other as if they would never let go. She had fallen asleep in his arms, their legs entwined, their bodies connecting. He had seen it as the beginning of their lives together as a couple.

When he had woken up alone the next morning, even that hadn't changed his belief. Wasn't she always up early? She was just letting him sleep. Nothing had prepared him for the crushing words she had spoken just a few minutes later.

But today had given him some hope. They had kissed as they were saying goodnight. Something he had been thinking of doing all day. It was just a little kiss, but tender and loving. A kiss that told him her emotions were the same as his. She couldn't hide her true feelings when they kissed.

It occurred to him that she may have agreed to join him in bed again if their kiss had become more intense. But friends with benefits was not a route he wanted to go down with Abby. He wanted her to choose him. To acknowledge that there was more to their relationship than just good friends. He was determined he would not be accepting anything less.

'I can't believe the six weeks are almost up,' Abby said the next morning. 'It seems only yesterday when you surprised me in the office.'

'I don't have to go,' Daniel said, surprising her again.

'What do you mean? You're going back on Wednesday.'

'I could extend my stay.'

'I thought you had a literary do to go to.'

'It's not a problem. I could attend online.'

'Daniel, you have to go back.'

'Why?'

'You need to test your feelings when you're back in Canada. Staying just friends could be the obvious choice.'

'Why do you keep insisting that I don't know what I want? I want my life to be wherever you are.'

'But your life is in Canada.'

'My life of one-night stands and wild parties?' he said bitterly. 'Whatever you've heard from others, that is not who I am.'

'Daniel, I know that. Of course I know that. I was talking about your friends, your home, your work.'

'I can write anywhere. And I can stay in touch with friends online. We're proof of that. I have no ties in Canada like the ones I have here.' But he felt he was getting nowhere. 'Have you still not worked out why I arrived three weeks early?' he asked.

'You said it was to write.'

'Yes, and that was true. But there was another reason.'

She stared at him, nervous of what he might say next. Reminders of that first week, when so much of their conversation had been about marriage, began to flash through her mind. Surely he wasn't going to propose?

But his explanation made no mention of marriage. 'I was becoming tired of our video chats. I wanted to be near you. Physically near you. There's absolutely no reason for me to go back next week. I can go back in December. With you.'

'Please, Daniel. Don't do this,' she said, begging him not to keep asking for what she wasn't ready to give.

Things had softened a little between them by the time they left for Beth's house, but Abby had an idea to bring some more fun back. As she turned into Meadow Way she parked the car at the top of the road. Daniel had not been expecting that. 'What's going on?' he asked.

'A trip down memory lane.' She pointed to a cherry tree on the other side, one of several that lined the whole street and made a spectacular display of pale pink blossom in the spring. 'Remember that tree?'

It suddenly dawned on him what was going to happen. A re-run of their race down the road. That particular tree had been their starting point, the one in front of Abby's house had been the finishing line.

'And I'm going to win fairly this time,' she said. 'They'll be no need for you to cheat like you did before.'

'I wouldn't dare,' he laughed, remembering the time

when he had been caught out. It had happened during the summer holidays when they were young teenagers. He had felt guilty that he would always win when they were at primary school together, so suggested they have another go when he had found out she was doing well in athletics at secondary school. But he had slowed down towards the end, feigning breathlessness, and let her overtake.

It had been a huge mistake. He hadn't fooled her at all, and she had been furious with him. 'How could you, Daniel,' she shouted, causing Beth to come out to see what was going on. 'I want to win because I'm faster, not because you let me.'

But that had never happened. She had managed to get close on the handful of times they had raced since then, but his winning streak had continued.

'You think you've still got it?' she teased, certain that she had the upper hand this time.

'Hundred per cent,' he replied, sounding far more confident than he felt. He played a lot less sport now than in his youth, spending far too much of his time behind a desk. Plus his muscles were aching after the seven-mile walk they had done only the day before. Nevertheless, he was ready to give it a try.

'On your marks, get set, go!' they shouted in unison, setting off down the road together. They were still close as they reached the bend, but Abby had energy in reserve and surged forward over the final few yards. There was absolutely nothing Daniel could do about it.

'Yes!' she cried, hitting the tree trunk triumphantly.

Daniel was definitely not faking this time. He leant forward with his hands on his knees, breathing heavily, watching Abby jumping up and down with seemingly endless amounts of energy.

'Congratulations,' he managed to say, still struggling with his breath.

She threw her arms around him as he straightened up, 'I was pretty good, wasn't I?'

'You were. And I was terrible. I should have made more use of that gym.'

Beth was standing in the doorway watching them. 'This brings back memories,' she smiled. 'But I don't remember Daniel making such a fuss when he won.'

'Mum, this is a big deal,' Abby said, walking up the driveway towards her. 'I've waited twenty-seven years for this.'

'Let her have her moment,' Daniel said to Beth. 'Next time I'll be better prepared, and she'll find herself back in second place.'

'In your dreams,' Abby laughed, still revelling in her victory.

He came up behind her, wrapping his arms around her waist, his head nestling against her neck as he walked her up the driveway. 'Which is where you'll always be,' he whispered in her ear.

THIRTY-ONE

The aromas of a roast dinner reached them from the kitchen as they walked down the corridor. 'It smells delicious, Beth. Is there anything I can do to help?' Daniel asked.

'Thank you, but no. It's all in hand. Can I get you something to drink?'

'Drink!' Abby shouted. 'I'd better go back and fetch the car.'

'What's that about?' Beth laughed as Abby disappeared out of the front door.

'She's just remembered we've left things in the car. And we left the car at the top of the road.'

It wasn't long before the doorbell announced Abby's return, the car now parked in the driveway. 'That was quick,' Daniel said as he opened the door.

'I ran all the way. Some of us still have plenty of energy left. Have you got your breath back yet?'

He rolled his eyes at her. 'Will you ever allow me to forget this?'

'No, never,' she laughed. 'I shall remind you of it when we're old and grey and reminiscing in the sunshine on a faraway beach.'

'And making new memories?'

'Of course!'

He gently moved a stray tendril of her hair back to its original position. 'Don't make me wait another thirty-five years, Abby.'

They stared at each other for several seconds, but she had no answer for him. She passed him the bouquet of flowers for Beth, then turned away and walked down the corridor clutching a bottle of white wine, Daniel following close behind.

Beth was delighted with the bouquet of roses and freesias. 'Oh, they're beautiful. Thank you so much.' she said, giving Daniel a hug. 'Your visit has gone so quickly. It's Wednesday you're leaving, isn't it?'

'That's right. Abby will be throwing me out early on Wednesday morning.' He had tried to keep his tone light, but it came out edged with sarcasm.

'Daniel, that's so unfair,' Abby said. 'Why would you say that?'

'It was meant as a joke. Although, actually, it is what you're doing, isn't it? You've certainly made it clear you don't want me to extend my stay.'

'And you know why.' She didn't want to argue in front of her mother. With a scathing look in Daniel's direction, she removed herself to the lounge.

'I'm sorry you had to hear that, Beth,' Daniel said, embarrassed at what had happened. 'I'm so frustrated with her refusal to compromise. But this isn't the place to bring it up.'

'I don't like seeing you both unhappy. Do you want to talk about it?'

'If it's alright with you, I think I just need some fresh air.'

'That's fine. Take as long as you need.'

He stepped through the back door and into the garden, walking past the window with his head down.

Beth went to join Abby.

'Is he angry with me?' Abby asked her.

'No, not angry. Frustrated is the word he used. He's taking a walk round the garden to clear his head. What's gone wrong, sweetheart?'

'He says he doesn't want to go back to Canada next week, and I say he has to. I couldn't bear it if he goes back with animosity between us, but we just can't agree. He wants to rush in without thinking first, and I can't do that when it's such a huge decision. I need to be a hundred per cent certain.'

'Can anyone ever be that certain?' Beth asked. 'If two people have fallen in love, sometimes they just need to take a leap of faith.'

'But we're constantly sniping at each another. I broke my own rules, and now I have no idea how to handle the fallout.'

'As long as you're honest with each other you'll find a way through this.'

'I hope so.' She gave Beth a sad smile. 'Please find me something to do. I need to be busy.'

They went back into the kitchen. 'You could put the flowers in a vase for me,' Beth said. 'Then keep an eye on the dinner, and I'll go and make sure Daniel's okay.'

Beth walked up the path to where Daniel was sitting. 'This was a favourite place for Adam and I,' she said as she sat down beside him on the stone bench. 'Early in the morning he would walk round the garden, then I would bring mugs of tea, and we'd sit and watch the sunrise together.'

'That's a wonderful memory to hold onto,' Daniel said.

'Yes, it is. And I still love to sit out here when the weather's nice. It's where I feel closest to Adam.'

'What do you think he would say about Abby and I getting together?'

'He would have no qualms about that as long as you were both happy. And neither would I. We always knew there was a strong connection between the two of you. You seemed to gel right from the start.'

'Yes, we did. But even now, after everything we've been through, she still wants us to stay just friends.'

'She doesn't want to be rushed into a decision, Daniel. I don't think she means to fight with you; she's fighting with herself. Just be patient with her.'

He gave a wry laugh. 'I'm doing my best.'

They heard footsteps on the path and both looked up as Abby walked towards them. 'Five more minutes,' she said.

'I'll go and finish off,' Beth said. 'You two stay and chat.'

'We won't be long,' Abby said, sitting down next to Daniel. 'Are you okay?' she asked.

'I'm fine. I just wish we could sort it out.'

'These past six weeks have flown by, Daniel. It's only a week or two longer until I come and visit you in Canada. It's no time at all.'

Yes, two months in Canada without her would not be a problem if that was all it took for her to come round to his way of thinking. But Daniel knew it was more complicated than that. What if those weeks apart were not enough for her to commit herself to him? What if she fell effortlessly back into the life she'd had before?

Was there really no alternative other than playing the waiting game? It was a game he had never been particularly good at.

THIRTY-TWO

'What time does the supermarket open?' Daniel asked Abby on Sunday morning.

'Eleven,' she said. 'Why? Are you thinking of going?'

'Yeah, I thought I'd make a bit of an effort tomorrow after all. I need to pick up some breakfast items.'

But it was already ten thirty. 'Can we go a bit later?' she asked. 'I'm nowhere near ready to go out. I've still got to shower and wash my hair.'

'Don't worry. I'll go on my own. I'd rather go now so I can try elsewhere if they don't have what I want.'

'Well, if you're sure.'

After Daniel had left, Abby took a quick shower, sorted out her hair, and within the hour was downstairs on the sofa with a cup of coffee and a book, dressed in a baggy sweatshirt and joggers.

She was suddenly interrupted by the buzzer. 'Did you forget your keys?' she asked, since it could only be Daniel.

But there was a pause at the other end. Then a voice said, 'It's me.'

Her recognition was instant, just as he had known it would be. 'Come on up,' she said, keeping her voice calm.

What else could she have done? There was no time to think. She was grateful that she'd had the foresight to get dressed.

She was waiting in the doorway as the lift doors opened, as he stepped out and back into her world. He kissed her on the cheek. 'It's good to see you, Abs.'

No-one ever called her Abs. Only Gavin.

She took him into the kitchen. 'I've made some coffee,' she said. 'Would you like a cup?'

'Thanks.' He gave her a smile. 'Have you missed me?'

But she wasn't falling for any of that nonsense. 'I'm intrigued to know why you're here.' There was no point in asking how he had found her address. In his line of work he would have no trouble getting that information.

'I had a sudden urge to see you,' he said. 'I'd like to take you to dinner at The Royal this evening.'

'No, that's impossible. I can't do that, Gavin.'

'Then we'll do lunch.'

'I'm not sure what I'm doing this afternoon.'

They were still standing by the coffee machine. She felt his hand on her waist as he moved closer. 'Please, Abs. Let me spend time with you. You must know how difficult it was to arrange.'

'Why don't you sit down,' she said, and he did as she asked. 'I might be able to do afternoon tea.'

'You are joking,' he laughed. 'That would be something more suited for my mother, not you and I.'

She shrugged. 'Then that's fine. We'll leave it.'

'No, we won't,' he said. 'If that's what you want to do,

then I'll take you.'

'I need to make a quick phone call.'

'Calling reinforcements?'

She ignored his comment and went into the hall. But she didn't make a call, she sent a two word text instead: *Gavin's here.*

Gavin was no longer at the island when she came back. He had taken his coffee and was standing in the dining room, looking out over the town. 'This is a great place,' he said as she came to join him.

'Yes, I love it.'

'Something like this would cost a fortune in Central London.'

'I suppose it would, but I'm happy living here. I'm not a city girl.'

'No.' He turned towards her. 'You're looking good, Abs. Beautiful, in fact.'

'In these clothes?' she said, laughing awkwardly.

'Why are you so nervous?' he asked. 'Relax. It's only me.'

'It was such a surprise, that's all.' She finally gave him a smile. 'But it is good to see you.'

'That's better,' he grinned. 'And who are we waiting for?'

'Daniel's staying with me at the moment.'

'Is he indeed? I thought he was writing a string of bestselling novels somewhere in the Canadian wilderness.'

'He still lives in Canada. He's over for a visit.'

'And this must be the man himself,' he said as they

heard the key in the lock.

They walked back to the kitchen. 'Danny-boy, how are you?' Gavin said, striding confidently towards him, hand outstretched.

Daniel took Gavin's hand and gave a firm handshake. 'Gavin. Still saving the world?'

'I do what I can.'

'And what are you doing here?'

'I'm here to take my charming ex-wife to The Royal. Does she need your permission?'

'Abby's her own woman,' Daniel said. 'She makes her own decisions.'

'It's for afternoon tea,' Abby explained, keen to avoid any misunderstandings. 'I wasn't sure if we had any plans.'

They had no plans, and Abby knew that. It was obvious to Daniel that she wanted to go. If she hadn't, she would have said so outright. All he had to do was invent some prior engagement, and she would have stayed. But he couldn't do that to her. 'No plans,' he said. 'You should go, if that's what you want.'

'You're welcome to join us,' Gavin said, certain that Daniel would never agree.

As predicted, Gavin's offer was immediately dismissed. 'You don't need me there,' Daniel said. 'I'm sure you have a lot of catching up to do.'

'What time do you want to leave?' Abby asked Gavin. 'Have you booked a table?'

'We'll leave whenever you're ready. It's flexible.'

'I'd better go and get changed.'

‘Shall I come and help?’ Gavin asked.

‘No, I can manage.’

‘What’s the problem?’ he grinned. ‘It’s nothing I haven’t seen before.’

‘Then you don’t need to see it again, do you?’ she said, disappearing up the stairs.

It wasn’t ideal to leave Daniel and Gavin alone for any length of time with their constant jibing, so she made quick decisions. A smart knee-length dress to complement Gavin’s suit, and a pair of diamond stud earrings to complete the look. She left her hair loose and added just a minimum of makeup.

Both men stood up as she walked through the open door, but Daniel reached her first. ‘It’s all fine,’ he said in a faint whisper. ‘You look lovely,’ he added, his voice returning to normal. Then he kissed her lightly on the lips. ‘Have a good time.’

‘Thank you,’ she said.

Daniel watched from the kitchen doorway as Gavin helped Abby on with her coat, then held open the front door for her. The perfect gentleman, immaculately dressed and well-groomed. He was well aware that Gavin would never be seen in unpressed clothes and with just-got-out-of-bed hair.

They said their goodbyes, and Daniel turned back to the kitchen. Sitting at the island, his head in his hands, his thoughts began to run wild. What was the real reason Gavin was here? Was it as innocent as he had made out? Was he expecting to take Abby to bed?

Daniel was convinced she wouldn't agree. He felt disloyal even considering it. But she had told him what had happened after their divorce. Would she see this as a similar occasion?

Why hadn't he thought of taking Abby to a meal at The Royal himself? It was less than twenty miles away. But it was too late now. Somehow Gavin had always managed to be one step ahead.

He left the flat fifteen minutes after Abby and Gavin, not wanting to stay alone with his thoughts, and made his way to the pub for a few games of pool. But he would make sure he was back at the flat before Abby returned.

THIRTY-THREE

'How's Beth?' Gavin asked as they left the town behind them.

'She's doing really well, thanks,' Abby said.

'I'm sorry I couldn't make the funeral.'

'She understood. And she appreciated the flowers you sent and your letter. Well, we both did. It was very thoughtful.'

'It was the least I could do,' he said. 'You know I would have been there if it had been at all possible.'

'Yes, I know.'

The hotel was enclosed within extensive grounds. But what had once been beautiful gardens, was now a golf course. Gavin drove up the winding road until they reached a stone archway leading into the hotel courtyard.

They were shown to a private table in the corner of the tearoom. Abby was enthralled by the pink and pale green colour scheme, the soft upholstered chairs, the unobtrusive piano playing. 'This is lovely,' she said as Gavin pulled out her chair.

The table was soon filled with the usual delights of afternoon tea. 'It all looks delicious,' Abby said, helping herself to an egg and watercress sandwich as Gavin poured the champagne.

'I can't believe I agreed to this,' he laughed. Then he held up his glass and Abby did the same. 'To happy reunions,' he said as they touched glasses.

'Is there anyone special in your life at the moment?' Abby asked.

'No. There is a woman I see on a fairly regular basis, but we're not exclusive. Since neither one of us is big on commitment, it suits us very well. How about you?'

'I like to date, but I'm not interested in long-term romance.'

'I hope our marriage didn't ruin the idea of romance for you.'

'I suppose the experience has made me more wary. But there are other things, too. My job, for instance.'

'And how's that going?'

She told him about the course. About how she wanted to move away from the negativity of divorce. She made him laugh with anecdotes from some of her more outrageous cases.

'I was never one of those cheaters, Abs. You do believe that don't you?' It was important to him that she did.

'Of course I do. Your self-discipline was always strong.'

'Over three years making love to just one woman. It's never happened before or since. You had an incredible hold on me.'

Wasn't that similar to what Daniel had said? How strange that they should think the same thing. It was not how she saw herself at all.

She caught him watching her and recognised the smile in his eyes. But he was going to be disappointed. 'We've had our Paulo Nutini moment, Gavin. It's not happening again.'

'Am I that obvious?'

'You are to me. Is that why you're here?'

'It's not the only reason. I'm enjoying your company. But I have the odd lonely night when I conjure you up in my thoughts. I have very fond memories of our last meeting. I think we set the benchmark for break-up sex.'

'Sex was never one of our problems.'

'And yet you're turning down the chance of one more night with me.'

'Yes, I am.'

She felt his eyes assessing her, searching for clues. 'You're in love with Danny-boy, aren't you?'

'Don't call him that. You know he hates it.'

'We enjoy winding each other up. It's just a harmless game we play. Contrary to what you may think, I actually have a lot of respect for him.'

She believed him. There had been times when he'd had to keep things from her, but he was always honest with what he did say.

'Are you going to answer the question?' he asked, although they were both aware it had been rhetorical.

She refused to betray Daniel by denying what they had together. 'Yes, I'm in love with him. But it's complicated.'

'Love is always complicated. That's why I tend to stay

away from it.'

'Why did you marry me?' she asked. A question she had never asked him before. Perhaps she had been afraid of his answer. Now that it no longer mattered, she was just curious to know.

He shrugged. 'Was I in love with you? At that moment, yes. Did I think it would last? No. But then, neither did you. We were in Vegas. It was a fun thing to do. An impulsive act that wasn't meant to be taken seriously.'

She stared down at her plate, digesting what Gavin had just said.

'Have I got that wrong?' he asked.

She was touched to hear the concern in his voice. She looked up at him, a sad smile on her face. 'No, not really. Maybe I took it a little more seriously than you did. But if I'm honest, deep down I knew it wasn't forever.' She was surprised by her words. It was something she had never admitted before. Not even to herself.

'Do you think you'll ever have another go?'

She shook her head. 'Marriage isn't in my plans for the future. I tried it once, and I wasn't very good at it. Maybe I'm better living on my own.'

'I can't believe that. Someone as amazing and beautiful as you deserves to be loved. I'm sorry it couldn't be me, but I gave it my best shot. It was the one thing in my life I messed up.'

'We both messed up,' she said. 'And we're not alone. I'm constantly dealing with husbands and wives who have messed up. Marriage is often far harder than people think it will be.' Then she smiled at him. 'But I'm glad I can sit here with you without any bitterness or resentment. There aren't many divorced couples who have that.'

'I'm glad, too,' he smiled, giving her hand a gentle squeeze.

On the drive back they chatted comfortably together, filling in the missing years without any intrusive questions.

Gavin insisted on accompanying Abby to her front door, but had no expectations of being asked into the flat. They said their goodbyes in the corridor.

'Thanks for seeing me, Abs,' he said, taking her in his arms and kissing her on the cheek. 'I shall miss you tonight.'

'You'll be fine,' she said, smiling up at him. 'And I had a lovely time. Thank you.'

'Good luck with Dan- with Daniel,' he said. 'He's one of the good guys.' Then he squeezed her hand once again. 'Be happy.'

'You too,' she said. 'And stay safe.'

'Of course,' he said softly, letting go of her hand and gently running his fingers down her arm.

He stepped into the lift and back out of her life. They smiled at each other as the lift doors closed. Would she ever see him again? She had no idea. But there were no longer any ties between them. He was part of her past. It was her present that she needed to focus on now. And her future.

She sat down on the floor by the front door, wanting to

settle her thoughts before she saw Daniel. Now that she had accepted that her marriage to Gavin was never meant to last, was she ready to embrace a romantic future with Daniel?

But what if a relationship between her and Daniel was also destined to end? Saying goodbye to him would be so much harder. He had been part of her life since she was six years old. She couldn't risk losing him. It was too much.

The door opened and Daniel came out. He sat down on the floor beside her. 'How was it?' he asked.

'Really nice. A gorgeous setting, and the food was wonderful.' She showed him the box in her hand. 'I brought a doggy bag back for you.'

'Thanks,' he said, taking it from her. 'And the company?'

'We got on well together. Definitely not your average divorced couple. But there's nothing between us, Daniel. Honestly. Gavin is just someone that I used to love. No more than that.'

'And who am I?'

'You are someone who I will always love. Someone who I will always want in my life.' She paused and rested her head against him. 'I just wish that could be enough for you.'

THIRTY-FOUR

The bacon and maple syrup combination that Daniel served up for breakfast on Canadian Thanksgiving Day was not something Abby would have chosen for herself. 'I'm used to my pancakes with strawberries and chocolate sauce,' Abby said. 'But it looks interesting.'

Daniel put a little taste of everything onto a spoon. 'Trust me, you'll love it. Open wide!'

She was surprised at how well the flavours went together. 'Hmm, it's actually very good.'

'What did I tell you?' he smiled. 'Could you manage some more?'

Her mouth was full, but she gave him a nod. He took a plate of pancakes and bacon from the oven where they had been keeping warm.

'You know, there's a lesson to be learnt here,' he said.

'And what's that?' she asked as she poured on the syrup.

'Mixing unintended things together can sometimes turn out to be the perfect combination.' Clearly he was no longer talking about pancakes.

'And you, Abby,' he continued. 'You could be my

Unmistakable Unintended.'

'Perhaps I could be,' she said softly, thinking out loud.

Had he heard her correctly? But she wasn't looking at him. She was staring straight ahead, lost in her thoughts. He wouldn't ask her to repeat it. He didn't want to be proved wrong.

'You look miles away,' he said instead.

She turned to face him with a smile. 'Sorry. It was your words. They were so beautiful.'

'Do you have two words for me?'

As she tucked into her pancakes her mind searched through the V's, but she didn't like what she found. There were so many unpleasant words beginning with V. She knew she would never be able to come up with two words as amazing as Daniel's.

She finally found two that fitted the occasion. 'Valuable Visitor,' she said. 'It has been really special having you here, Daniel.'

'Thanks.' He managed a smile, although it was clear to him that she hadn't changed her mind. She wasn't going to ask him to stay. But he refused to give up hope. They still had one more day.

Daniel woke up the next morning with Abby asleep on his lap. Thanksgiving Day had ended in the early hours of the morning after two televised Canadian Football games. Unsurprisingly, Abby hadn't managed to last the course. Sixty minutes of actual game time turned into almost three hours of real time, and that was only the first game.

She had started to yawn, but didn't want to leave Daniel on his own. So she had curled up with her head on a cushion on his lap, and fallen asleep. There were no complaints from Daniel.

When he had finally switched off the TV, he pulled one of the throws over her, then fell asleep himself. But his position wasn't as comfortable as Abby's, and he had woken up first.

A short time later, Abby began to stir. She stretched herself out and opened her eyes, at first disorientated.

'It's okay, we're still on the sofa,' Daniel said, and Abby sat up.

'What time is it?' she asked.

'Almost eleven o'clock.'

'In the morning? Oh dear,' she giggled.

He hugged her to him, wanting her to stay in his arms.

But Abby was ready to get up. 'I need a shower,' she said. And she left him with his thoughts.

There were no plans for Daniel's last day other than to spend it together. They had a late lunch, then took one last walk by the river to watch the sunset on Adam's bench. Daniel refused to see the setting of the sun as symbolising the end of his hopes of a relationship with Abby. He pictured it as a romantic backdrop which would give him one final opportunity to convince her that it was worth taking a chance on love.

'It's been an amazing six weeks,' she said, leaning her head against him. 'The highs have easily outshone the lows. I've had a wonderful time.'

'So we agree on something. Don't let it slip away from us, Abby.'

'There are so many conflicting thoughts and emotions swirling round my head. You have to give me the chance to sort through them.'

'Just let them go. All you need are your feelings for me.'

'I do love you, Daniel. But it's not as simple as that.'

'It is if you're willing to let go of what's holding you back and focus on the important things. What you went through with Gavin has no bearing on our relationship. And statistics don't matter, either for or against. They are no more relevant to our lives than the characters in my novels. And neither are the experiences of your clients. We're all individuals who make our own choices.'

He placed his fingers gently under her chin and turned her face towards him. 'And I choose you.'

His words warmed her heart and brought tears close to the surface, but her concerns had not completely dissolved. 'It just seems an impossible dream,' she said.

'But it isn't. If you choose me, it can be our reality.'

'It's too soon, Daniel. We need to see how we feel after a few weeks apart.'

'So that's it? You won't even consider it?'

'That's not what I said. I'll come and visit you in December as we planned, and we can talk things through then.'

They were going round in circles. He was out of ideas. What choice did he have other than to respect her wishes?

The six weeks were up. In spite of his best efforts, he had not managed to achieve what he had set out to do. The realisation hit him hard. For the first time in his life, he felt a complete failure.

Daniel had a hire car delivered to the flat within an hour of returning from their walk. After the conversation they'd had by the river, he felt there was no alternative other than to drive himself to the airport.

'That makes sense,' Abby said when he told her what he'd done. 'The traffic will be horrendous on the way back. It will be so much easier for me to come home on the train.'

There was a cheerfulness to her voice that Daniel took exception to. It was false bravado on her part. An attempt to cover up the hurt she was feeling at his imminent departure. But he failed to see beyond his own pain, and his reply came out harsher than he intended.

'Where did you get the idea that you were coming to the airport? That's not happening.'

'But I always see you off at the airport.'

'Not this time, Abby. You need to respect my opinion on this. Saying goodbye in the morning or at the airport would be a nightmare for me, and I refuse to put myself through it. I won't be changing my mind.'

'So you don't want to see me tomorrow?'

'I'd rather leave quietly. There'll be no point in you getting up early.'

He saw the look of horror on her face and softened his

voice. 'I need you to support me on this, Abby.'

'Of course. If that's what you want.' She turned away, willing the tears not to fall.

'I'll go and pack,' he said, retreating to his room.

She had never felt more alone. How had it come to this? Remembering the joy she had felt on his arrival, it seemed inconceivable that just six weeks later her world was falling apart.

THIRTY-FIVE

Abby sat alone in the kitchen, unsure whether Daniel would come back or just go straight to bed. Her mind went back to the day of Daniel's arrival. Hadn't she known from the start that there had been something different about this visit?

Over the past six weeks they had been given a glimpse of what their lives could be together. But how could she be sure that what they had found would last? Silent tears began to fall, and she wiped them away. It all seemed so hopeless.

She was still sitting where Daniel had left her when he came out of his room an hour later.

'The packing's more or less done,' he said.

'What time will you be leaving tomorrow?'

'About five. Check-in doesn't close until half seven, so that should give me plenty of time. Shall we finish off the wine?'

'Yes, okay.'

He handed her a glass then sat down beside her. Her eyes gave away the fact that she had been crying.

'Did you think I wasn't coming back? I wouldn't do

that to you.'

'I'd almost convinced myself that you would.'

'You do understand why we have to say goodbye tonight, don't you?'

'Yes. And you're right. It would be a lot more emotional than it's been before. For both of us.'

'If you started crying at the airport, it would start me off.'

'It's okay to show emotion, Daniel.'

'I think I've been through every bloody emotion there is in these six weeks. But it's all been worth it, Abby. And I mean that.'

'More wonderful memories.'

'Yeah,' he said, his voice tinged with sadness. He took hold of her hand. 'Thanks for letting me love you, Abby.'

Touched by his words, she stood up and stepped into the comfort of his arms. Would she ever be able to sort through the confusion in her head?

Daniel was the first to pull away. 'I need to get some sleep.'

They stopped outside his bedroom door one last time and hugged again, their lips coming together for a quick kiss. 'I'll call you when I get back,' he said.

'I'll be waiting. Have a safe journey.'

'I'll be fine.'

But she wasn't ready to let him go. She put her arms around his neck and pulled his head towards her for one more kiss, this time surprising them both by pushing her tongue between his lips. For a brief moment he allowed himself to enjoy the sensation once again, until he came to his senses and broke their connection.

'Abby! What the hell are you doing?'

'I just needed to kiss you.'

'Like that?' he shouted. 'Are you saying you want me to stay?'

She looked down at the floor. Was that what she was saying? But she was unnerved by his reaction and hesitated for too long.

'No, of course you're not,' he said, still angry with her. 'I'm not kissing you like that so you can reject me again. I'm tired of being made a fool of.'

'Please, Daniel', she said desperately. 'I didn't mean-'

He wouldn't let her finish. 'Let's not make this any harder, Abby,' he said, his voice a lot calmer. 'I don't need another apology.' He took her face in his hands, his thumbs gently wiping away the few tears that had escaped. 'I know you're hurting, too,' he said. 'But we will get through this.'

She nodded, too emotional to speak. He kissed her on the forehead. 'I'll see you in December.' Then he vanished into his room, closing the door behind him.

Why had she handled things so badly? It was so hard to do or say the right thing when they were riding the crazy rollercoaster of emotions. She turned off the lights and made her way upstairs to what Daniel called her sanctuary.

As she lay in bed her mind refused to settle. Was it really going to be enough for her to go back to seeing him on a screen? Should she ask him to stay? She set her alarm for ten past four; that would give her one more chance to speak to him. Now that she had a plan she felt far more positive. It wasn't long before sleep finally came.

Daniel had one more task to do before he could finally get to bed. At the bottom of the wardrobe he found a box that he had brought with him from Canada. A white box with pink ribbon, a gift tag and a card. He had known weeks ago what he would write on the card if his plans had not gone as hoped. And here he was, at the end of his visit, with his plans and his hopes shattered.

From memory he wrote down his chosen words, then tucked the card under the gift in the box and tied the box with ribbon. The words on the gift tag had only been decided a couple of days ago, but were perfect for the occasion.

He wasn't proud of the way he had spoken to Abby earlier that night, and then again when they were saying goodbye. But the way she kept blowing hot and cold made it impossible for him to hide the pain and frustration he was feeling.

The gift would show her that his feelings and his love for her were genuine. That he wanted to share the rest of his life with her. It would remind her how much they had meant to each other over the years they had been friends. And help her decide to take the next step.

Daniel was awoken by his alarm just a few hours later. He put it on snooze for ten minutes, then got up and was ready to leave in twenty. He didn't stop to make himself a coffee. But he went into the kitchen and left his gift on the worktop.

Back in the hall, he paused by the stairs and said a silent goodbye to Abby. Then he manoeuvred his way through the front door with two suitcases and a backpack, letting the door shut behind him.

THIRTY-SIX

The sudden noise of the front door closing jolted Abby awake. She had no idea what had awoken her. Her body lay motionless, her ears alert for any further sound. Only silence reached her. She checked the time: nearly four o'clock. She hadn't missed her alarm.

As she lay in the darkness she thought through her decision and knew it was the right one. The overwhelming emotion she was feeling was love. Deep and precious and all-consuming love. They had found a level of passion with each other that they had both failed to find with anyone else. How could she possibly be with anyone else now that Daniel had loved her?

Why had she been so stubborn? Her rules had been made because of the failure of her marriage and the experiences of her clients. They had nothing to do with her relationship with Daniel. Wasn't that what he had been trying to tell her?

And yet even when those rules had been broken she had continued to deny the relationship that was theirs for the taking. Instead of embracing it and exploring it further, she had turned away.

But now she was going to put things right. She was going to choose him. Not in two or ten or twenty years' time. She was going to choose him today. Today would be the first day of their new lives together.

She jumped out of bed as her alarm went off, and was dressed and ready to go downstairs within ten minutes. This was definitely not the day for taking her time. She had to see Daniel and ask him to stay. Had to tell him he had been right all along. That he was her one true love. That it was far too late for them to stay just good friends.

She called out his name as she ran down the stairs, but there was no response. The hall was in darkness. Nothing was making sense. She switched on the light and made her way to Daniel's room, her pace slowing as her heart beat increased. She stopped in the open doorway, unsettled by the silence. 'Daniel?' she whispered. Her quiet questioning received no audible answer, just a neat and tidy room that in itself spoke volumes.

Unable to accept what she was seeing, she stepped inside and went through the pointless exercise of opening the wardrobe, the drawers, even checking the en suite. But no trace of him remained. Only emptiness stared back at her.

She sank down onto the bed, her head in her hands. *Please tell me it's not true. Please tell me I'm not too late.* Her prayers were answered. There was plenty of time before his flight left. There was still another option. She ran back upstairs, picked up her phone and called him. To her horror, she discovered that his phone was switched off.

He had left and shut down her one remaining link to him.

Deflated and alone, she made her way back downstairs. Collapsing onto Daniel's bed, she grabbed one of the pillows and hugged it tightly. It was still full of the scent of him, bringing back memories of the night they had spent together in this room. In this bed. One blissful night she had spent in his arms.

The reality of what she had lost hit her head-on. This time he wasn't there to hold her against him as her tears spilled out in uncontrollable sobs.

Daniel stopped at a service station about halfway through his journey. He had no appetite, but bought himself a coffee for now and a chocolate bar for later. There was a newspaper on the table that someone had left behind. He did nothing more than glance at the headlines.

All he could think about was Abby. He regretted the way they had said goodbye last night, but it had been impossible to disguise the pain of her rejection.

She may have found his gift by now if she had woken up early in the hope of seeing him before he left, as he thought she might. That was why he had left an hour earlier than planned. He couldn't put himself through another goodbye.

He would have loved to have been a fly on the wall when she opened the box. To see her reaction first-hand. See her eyes sparkling with happy tears, her smile warming his heart. Or had he got it wrong yet again? Would she be flinging his gift across the room? No, that wasn't Abby's style. She would put the lid back on and push it aside. Not even notice the card he had written.

Why was he tormenting himself like this? He sipped his coffee and took another look at the paper. Flipping it over, he read through the sports pages in an attempt to focus his mind elsewhere.

Abby stayed on Daniel's bed, drifting in and out of sleep, for almost an hour. Eventually she pulled herself up, still clutching his pillow, and made her way into the kitchen. She was astonished to see a package waiting for her on the kitchen worktop. A white box, about eight inches square, tied with a bow in pink satin ribbon and with a pink glitter gift tag attached.

She picked it up and read the two-word message on the tag: *Wistful Wishes*. It brought a much-needed smile to her face. She gave the box a little shake. Something soft. She had no idea what to expect as she carefully untied the bow and lifted the lid. Inside were two cute little beanbag horses with red collars. White horses. It could only refer to one thing, surely?

Then she noticed an envelope at the bottom of the box with her name on it. She opened it up, her hands shaking as she read the card inside: *To my AA, whenever you're ready, bring the dress and meet me under the stars. Forever yours, DD x*

There was no doubt in her mind what it all meant. He was proposing in his own unique and special way. Taking her back to the first time they had talked about marriage over twenty-five years ago. He was wonderful. Amazing.

And she was not going to let him go.

It was over an hour's drive to Heathrow. But if she left right now, it might be possible to get there before check-in closed. The least she could do was try.

THIRTY-SEVEN

Driving as fast as she dared down the motorway, Abby was angry with herself for not finding the box sooner. Daniel would have known the first thing she did when she came downstairs was go into the kitchen and put the coffee on. That was why he had left the box there.

She had wasted so much time, and time was in short supply. It was only when she was driving through the tunnel underneath the runway that it occurred to her she would need extra time to park the car. This was not the movies. There would be no conveniently placed parking spot right in front of the airport departure doors so she could rush in with seconds to spare and fall straight into his arms.

Of course, the chances that he hadn't gone through check-in by now were extremely slim. But she clung to the idea that she would be able to get a message through to him.

In fact, check-in for Daniel's flight was still open and he had only just arrived. He had lost track of time at the service station and arrived twenty minutes before check-in closed. He stood a couple of feet away from the desk, reluctant to go ahead. There was no queue. Only himself and his thoughts. His primary thought was how on earth could he put himself thousands of miles away from Abby once again? Why didn't he wait for her answer in England?

He became aware of someone saying his name, and realised the woman at the desk was trying to get his attention. 'Check-in will be closing shortly for this flight, Mr Stratton.'

'Thank you,' he said, making no move towards her.

'Are you waiting for someone?' she asked.

Wasn't that precisely what he should be doing? Waiting. Not leaving. He would return to the hotel. Abby would be free to make her own decision without his interference.

And he knew what that decision would be. Hadn't he always known from the moment of that early morning birthday kiss? What he didn't know was how long she would resist her feelings. He would have to learn a new skill. He would have to learn to be patient. There was no other choice.

'I won't be flying today,' he said. 'I'd like to change my ticket.'

She gave him a warm smile. 'Of course,' she said, directing him to the appropriate desk.

Abby finally made it to check-in, but it was no surprise to her that she was too late. The flight had closed. She looked round frantically for a member of staff, anyone who could help her get a message through to the departure lounge. Instead, her eyes landed on someone totally unexpected.

Someone who never failed to surprise her.

She stared in amazement before he was swallowed up again by the crowd. But she had seen enough to know for certain that it was Daniel. Daniel with two suitcases? He wasn't leaving? She could scarcely believe it. And he was talking on his phone. She quickly sent him a message.

Daniel finished his call and saw there was a message from Abby: *I'm here.*

Was this really happening? It felt surreal. Where was she? He tried to spot her amongst the crowd. But he wasn't looking in the right direction.

She caught sight of him again, standing with his back towards her. She sent him another message: *Turn round.*

He did as she asked, and his eyes found her standing about thirty feet away. Looking so beautiful and turning his heart into mush as usual. But why was she here? He didn't dare hope too much. Didn't dare hope that his proposal would get a yes.

They ignored the hectic bustle of the airport carrying on around them and stood rooted to the spot, lost in their own private world. Neither one of them wanting to make a wrong move. People were walking continuously between them, blocking their view of each other. Still they stayed where they were, finding one another again each time a gap appeared.

Then Abby sent another message, this time the next two words of their game: *X X*

Daniel's face broke into a grin when he saw it. She was sending him kisses? Now that had to be a good sign. He made the first move to close the space between them, still grinning as he saw her warm and welcoming smile.

'Does that count?' she asked as he reached her side.

'It's perfect.' He took hold of her hand and kissed her gently on the lips. Twice.

She couldn't stop smiling. 'You didn't go.'

'I couldn't do it. I couldn't put thousands of miles between us again. I've booked myself back in at the hotel.'

'You're full of surprises, Daniel. I love that about you. And your present was amazing. Amazing and thoughtful and kind and beautiful. Just like you.' She hesitated, and once again he could hear the unspoken 'but' in her voice.

'It's okay, you can tell me,' he said softly.

She didn't want to hurt him, but she had to be honest. 'I love you so much, but I don't want to keep giving you false hope. I'm still not ready for marriage. I'm not sure if I'll ever be ready to go through that again. I'm scared it could jinx what we've found.'

'It's not all about marriage, Abby. It's about being together. Sharing our lives every day. Being soul mates as well as best friends. You can have all the time you need to think things through. I can wait.'

She shook her head, still not quite believing how close she had come to letting him go. 'No, you don't understand. I don't need time.' And then she told him the three words he had been longing to hear. 'I choose you.'

He wrapped his arms around her and held her close. She could hear his heart beating, and knew it was matching hers perfectly. 'Please stay with me,' she whispered.

He took out his phone and sent the next two word message: *You? Yes.*

For the first time they had reached the penultimate letter of the alphabet. But there was no way she would be able to think of another two words. In contrast to her calm exterior, her head was spinning. Her mind refused to focus.

'I don't have any Z's ready. I didn't think past those two X's.'

'Who needs Z's? This isn't an ending, is it?'

'No,' she smiled. 'This is a new beginning.'

'My Adorable Abby,' he laughed, hugging her to him once again.

At that moment she had no idea whether or not marriage would be in their future. But what she did know, without even a flicker of doubt, was that what they had together was real and unbreakable.

She wasn't naïve enough to think that things would always run smoothly, that there would be no further disagreements along the way. But their love and their trust were strong enough to see them through, whatever life threw at them.

They were two of the lucky ones. They had uncovered that elusive forever love. And nothing was more important than that.

EPILOGUE

Two Years Later

There had been changes in their lives over the past two years: Daniel had moved into Abby's flat; they had spent two Christmases together in Canada; Abby had qualified as a couples' therapist; Daniel's novel *Chaotic Contradictions* had been published; and Beth had come home from her first Christmas cruise with a sparkle in her eyes.

Abby had spent the night in her old room at her childhood home. She had gone to bed late, staying up and talking with Beth until two in the morning.

When Abby came downstairs, Beth was in the kitchen making tea. 'Are you okay, Mum?' she asked. 'Did you get enough sleep?'

'Yes, I'm fine. Quite excited, actually. I just need some time in the garden. We're on schedule, aren't we?'

'Yes, you go ahead. I'll come and fetch you if I need to.'

Beth picked up her mug of tea and carried it into the garden. She still liked to sit on the garden bench whenever she could. And today it was important to her that she made the time.

Half an hour later, Abby walked down the garden path to join her mum. 'Aunty Holly just phoned. They'll be here in a few minutes.'

Beth stood up and took hold of Abby's hand. 'I'm ready,' she smiled.

As they walked back to the house, they heard a car pull into the drive and went out of the side gate to meet Beth's sister, Holly, and Holly's husband, Jack. The one who Beth had chosen to walk her down the aisle.

'It seems like only yesterday when you were following *me* down the aisle,' Holly said to Abby.

'I've never forgotten that day,' Abby smiled. 'It was a very special moment in my life. And I'm sure today is going to be another of those special days.'

It was to be a small wedding in the local church, with only close family and friends. And the three bridesmaids – Abby, Holly, and Mike's daughter, Eleanor – would be wearing off-the-shoulder dresses in blush pink satin.

Beth was radiant in her ivory chiffon and lace dress. 'You look beautiful,' Abby told her, squeezing her hand and kissing her softly on the cheek, before leaving her in the capable hands of Jack.

Abby met up with Daniel at the church. After the ceremony and the photos, the wedding party moved on to a small reception in a private room at The Waterfront. And The Waterfront was where they would all be staying that night.

In the evening there was a big party for other family

members and friends in the hotel's main function room.

'It's been an amazing day,' Abby said to Daniel. 'I can't believe how smoothly everything went. No hiccups at all.'

'No tears?'

'There were a lot of tears last night, but not today.'

They watched Beth and her new husband dancing across the floor, smiling and laughing together, eyes only for each other.

'They look good together,' Daniel said.

'They do. I'm so happy for her. For both of them.' Then she took hold of Daniel's hand. 'Do you want to come outside for a while? It's getting a bit stuffy in here.'

They walked out onto the deserted patio and sat down on one of the sofas.

'It's such a beautiful evening,' Abby said, looking up at the night sky.

'I remember a little girl who dreamt of a night like this.'

'She's still here,' she said with a smile.

Daniel knew there could never be a more perfect moment. 'Have I told you how gorgeous you look in that dress?'

'You have, but I'll never tire of hearing it.'

'You look stunning.' Then he paused. 'But…'

There was a 'but'? She had no idea what was going on. Until his next words told her everything.

'…it lacks a bit of sparkle.'

Her heart began to beat faster.

Still holding her hand, he bent down on one knee. 'Marry me, Abby.'

Her smile was dazzling. 'You? Yes.'

'My Adorable Abby,' he laughed. 'What took you so long?'

They both stood up, and he swung her round in his arms. Setting her back on her feet, he produced a diamond ring from his trouser pocket. 'How about this?' he grinned, slipping it onto her finger. 'Is it sparkly enough for you?'

She stared at the ring in astonishment, then flung her arms around him. 'Daniel, it's perfect! When did you plan this?'

'I was going to propose to you tonight in our room. But I couldn't let an opportunity like this pass us by.'

He took her face in his hands, gently kissing the tears away.

The guitar intro from *Love you 'till the end* reached them from inside. 'They're playing our song,' he said.

'Are they? I didn't know we had a song,' she giggled.

'We do now,' he said softly, kissing her again. 'And if I remember correctly, we still have one more thing on our favourite little girl's dream list.'

She rested her head against him. 'You make all my dreams come true,' she whispered, and he held her close as they danced under the stars.

ABOUT THE AUTHOR

Five years ago, having reached a crossroads in her life, Alice chose an unexplored path and decided to run with her dreams.

As a result, she has completed her first novel: *from Adorable to You*

It has been an enjoyable and emotional journey, full of stresses and self-doubt, but – more importantly – a lot of fun!

ACKNOWLEDGMENTS

To my amazing group of family and friends who took an interest in my writing and listened patiently to my constant ramblings and ideas, a big thank you for your love and support.

Huge thanks to TC and Pushpa for taking the time to read my drafts and passing on their invaluable feedback.

And special thanks to Jay for being my sounding board at the start, and encouraging me to take that first step on my romance writing journey.

Printed in Great Britain
by Amazon

60147806R00143